THE NAKED HOUSE

FIVE PRINCIPLES FOR A MINIMALIST HOME

MOLLIE PLAYER

Copyright (C) 2020 Mollie Player

Layout design and Copyright (C) 2020 by Next Chapter

Published 2020 by Reality Plus – A Next Chapter Imprint

This book is a work of fiction. Names, characters, places, and incidents are the product of the author's imagination and have been used fictitiously. Any resemblance to actual events, locales, or persons, living or dead, is purely coincidental.

All rights reserved. No part of this book may be reproduced or transmitted in any form or by any means, electronic or mechanical, including photocopying, recording, or by any information storage and retrieval system, without the author's permission.

Photos by Brittany Van Horne. Visit her at facebook.com/BrittanyVanHornePhotography/

For more by Mollie Player, see her Amazon book page and MolliePlayer.com.

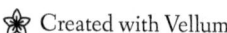 Created with Vellum

For my family, whom I both greatly convenience and badly annoy by employing the tactics in this book

1

THE NAKED HOUSE

YOUR HOUSE IS LIKE A PERSON; it has a soul

The other day, I read the craziest thing. Not crazy in the hyperbolic sense, either—actually a bit crazy. And you know what? Part of me believes it anyway.

It was in the book *Zero Limits* by spirituality writer Joe Vitale, and the words came from the guru who is the subject of said book. His name is Hew Len, and according to him, he has regular two-way interactions—yes, entire conversations—with all sorts of inanimate objects. My favorite line of his, said of a shabby hotel conference room: "This room says its name is Sheila."

I know, I know: that's what I thought, too. Still, this isn't an entirely novel belief. Only a few weeks before reading *Zero Limits* I read the book *Seth Speaks: The Eternal Validity of the Soul* by Jane Roberts, which discusses something similar. Seth is the spirit entity channeled by the author back in the 1960s, and the supposed true author of this and several of Roberts' other books. I figure that anyone who lives in another plane of existence deserves a fair hearing, and because of this I'm tempted to believe him when he says things like, "There is consciousness even in a nail ..."

Okay, so you might not be as susceptible to mysticism as I am. And trust me when I say I'm not trying to convert you or anything. I share these quotes simply because doing so makes me feel a bit less kooky when I make the first major philosophical statement of this book, namely: *your house is like a person; it has a soul.*

Your house is a kindly grandmother or an accomplished musician. It's a garbage collector or a playful child or an artist. It has an identity and it has a personality, and when you spend time with it, that personality is communicated. It is felt.

Your house is like a person. It has a soul. And that soul can, like a good book, be a friend.

Beauty is actually pretty important

Every time you walk through the front door of your home—or anyone's home, for that matter—your mood changes immediately. As soon as you take in the entrance and the first room, your levels of enjoyment, comfort and peace shift in subtle ways. Because that's what happens to us all when we enter a new space: we take on a little bit of its message. This is why people spend even more money on venue and decorations for a party than they spend on music and food. Being around people you love is great, and you can probably enjoy them anywhere. But being somewhere nice with those same people is much, much nicer. It's worth the extra money, the extra effort.

THE NAKED HOUSE

People often ask why other people like to go camping. The answer is obvious: the beauty. It's not the hiking, or the swimming, or the campfire with the s'mores (though I love all these things)—you can get those at a cabin. It's the feeling of waking up in the morning smelling truly fresh air and stumbling to the bathroom surrounded by trees. It's making coffee and pancakes outside, in one of the many places on the earth that are absolutely perfectly designed, exactly as they are.

No French doors. No balcony. No granite counter tops and tile back splashes. No fountain-like bathroom taps; you'll use a water pump that splashes your feet. No gables. No Great Grain Number Three from Sherwin Williams. No microfiber. No just-finished maple hardwood floors. Just nature.

And it's stunning. Every part of it. Everywhere you look. The birds in the trees, the spider on the log. The dirt is everywhere, and the dirt is wonderful. You wouldn't think of covering it up or getting rid of it, except inside the tent.

This is why you walked three miles with the heaviest backpack you've ever carried or packed your car to the brim, drove a long distance and spent two hours arranging your campsite. This is why you used an outhouse this morning and why you ate dehydrated food for dinner last night. This. Just this. Just the beauty.

Was it worth it? It is for me.

Beauty is important. Beauty makes you feel good. It brings peace. It makes you happier. Of course, our homes will never be beautiful in the way that nature is beautiful. But think about how you feel when you walk into your house every day. Is it a good feeling? If it is, is it as good as it could be? If not, why? What do you want to change?

Let's talk about your goal

Soon, I'll list the five principles of the Naked House. But first, let's talk for a second about what we're really doing when we're doing all this organizing. What is your goal? What are you moving toward? What do you want your home to make you feel?

When I asked myself that question, the answer was obvious. I didn't want a fancier house, or a bigger house, or even a sunnier, more cheerful one. I just wanted my house to feel peaceful. Home is where we relax. It's where we go to calm down. I like feeling cheerful, and I understand that some people love yellow kitchens and light blue bathrooms. This isn't what I wanted, though. I wanted brown. I wanted a muted color palette with very few adornments and an emphasis on the view from our large windows. I wanted my house to look like part of the earth.

Is that what you want, too? Do you want more serenity, simplicity and restfulness in your life? If so, the tips in this book might help. Because here, we're not just talking about home decor, or cleaning, or organization. What we're talking about is changing our environment in a way that allows for a fresh new perspective on life.

We're talking about how to be happier.

Of course, a serene look might not be your goal. You might want a more high-energy look. That's fine. But consider adding to your vision the element of peace. I contend that even a brighter home with more detail than mine has can benefit from some degree of minimalism.

Whatever look you desire, take a moment before starting your cleaning process to clearly visualize it. Then, if you get discouraged as you work through your rooms, you'll have a goal image to recall.

Life is hard. Reorganizing isn't.

The good news is that you can, of course, make these changes. Even without spending any money, there's a lot you can do. Behavior change is hard. Character change is really hard. Emotional change is even harder than that. But reorganizing your house? Not hard. Just takes time. Put on a good podcast and it can even be fun. If your brain is telling you otherwise, remind it that it's just one step. You're not doing it all in a day. You're cleaning one shelf, one corner, one area first, and you have a designated box (or two or three) for all the stuff that gets displaced. That box isn't your job right now. That box is for another day. Today, it's just this shelf, this corner. And when you're done, your life will be that much simpler for a good amount of time to come.

There are things in life that are genuinely hard, genuinely suck. Organizing isn't one of them. It's easy.

A brief word on other kinds of clutter

Some people have a difficult time getting rid of their favorite things. Other people enjoy doing so, but lack the time. If you're the former type, I suggest that you do what you can and pray for grace for the rest. Many experts suggest that the good feelings you get from letting go of the first few things you let go of (the feelings of freedom and self-care) often help inspire you to continue.

For the latter group, a different solution might be needed. Remember, clutter isn't only in your house; it can be in your life, too. Is there anything you can nix? Anything you can cut back on? Is it possible that at times, you're afraid of not being busy enough—of being bored? If so, you're in good company: I detest boredom. But I've learned to busy myself in more flexible ways. Instead of taking on a volunteer project or convincing myself I need to work a bit more, earn a bit more money, I come up with time-consuming hobbies that feed me. There's always something to do, but there's rarely a deadline. This is how I declutter my busy life.

Another kind of clutter: mind clutter. This one will kill you. If you're experiencing guilt, regret, anxiety, depression or frequent negativity, please seek help as soon as you can. You don't deserve that. No one does. It's garbage.

What, then, is the Naked House?

Okay, then. Let's get to it. The Naked House is, in five words, ordered from most important to least:

1. Bare;
2. Organized;
3. Matching;
4. Clean; and
5. Quality.

And really, that's it—the Naked House philosophy in a nutshell. Our homes may have souls, or they may not, but either way the mood they convey affects us. And a house that has all or most of these five traits is the one that I believe helps us find the inner calm that we seek.

In this book we will tour the Naked House room by room, noticing how these concepts are applied. First, though, an overview of each of these five principles in turn.

The Naked House is bare; or, The solution is almost always fewer things

When it comes to making your home a more peaceful place, the solution is almost always fewer things. That's not the only place in this book I'm going to make that statement, and there's a good reason for that: the first and most important principle of the Naked House is that it's bare. (That's why it's called "naked," after all.) And so, the question becomes: what exactly do I mean by this term?

Well, what is the image you have in your mind when I use the word "bare"? Is it a room that is completely empty, as if no one lives there at all? Or is there a couch and a few chairs, maybe even a vase with some flowers? For the purposes of this book, the terms "bare" and "naked" aren't so much about wearing no clothes as they are about wearing nothing that distracts from your beauty.

It is the complete absence of clutter.

Things don't cost what they cost

It's as true of a blender as it is of a dog: things don't cost what they cost. They cost what they cost to buy, maintain, move around and store. All these factors cost money (yes, space alone costs money: square footage is the number one factor in home price, and have you seen your heating bill lately?), but there are several other costs to consider, and both are more valuable than cash. The first is the cost of your time: the sheer number of minutes that add up to hours that add up to days that you spend rearranging, cleaning, protecting, and working around your stuff. And the second is the cost of your emotion.

In the home I grew up in, the kitchen cupboards were a mess. Because of that, it seemed that no matter which pan I needed, it was always on the bottom. This was annoying. Only slightly annoying, maybe, but multiply that experience by as many similar ones that you have throughout an average week in your home due only to clutter, and you'll have begun to calculate the emotional cost that I'm talking about. Contrast that with your daily experience in the Naked Home, where there is a place for everything and everything in its place—at least most of the time.

And, of course, it's not just the hassle of finding stuff that bothers us about our junk; it's the very existence of it at all. It's the visual distraction, the constant feeling of overwhelm that motivates most people to start their spring cleaning tradition.

Yet, most of us still vastly underestimate the significance of this emotional cost. Though we know we prefer the look of clean, open space, we rarely realize how much difference the presence or absence of each individual item will make.

THE NAKED HOUSE

Here's a simple exercise: picture a beautiful living room, with perfect flooring and beautiful paint and just a few couches, a lamp table and a lamp. Now imagine you can see the lamp cord trailing along part of one wall. And oh—there's a book lying on the arm of the couch, and a water glass on the lamp table, and a dog toy in the middle of the floor.

You get the point. The truth is—well, okay, far be it from me to use a lofty word like "truth," but the facts as I see them, are this: most people use unnecessary decorative items in their homes—wall hangings, knick-knacks, fully loaded bookshelves and the like—to camouflage the mess that lives alongside it—to justify its existence, so to speak.

Now, it doesn't happen in that order, of course. More often we start with the decorative stuff, then add the mess and clutter later on. However, if there were never piles of clothes on the bed and piles of dishes in the sink and piles of paperwork on the dining room table, eventually we might realize that the knick-knacks aren't adding to our pleasure in our homes, but rather taking it away ... and slowly, we'd begin to clear them out.

Here are a few of the larger items that I've pruned away over the years in order to bring out the natural, unadorned beauty of my simple, one-story home:

- Blinds and heavy drapes;
- Books (for now, most are stored in the garage);
- Stand-alone shelves and bookcases;
- Wall hangings, for the most part;
- Living room and dining room lamps and lamp tables;

- Kitchen appliances of various types;
- Bed frames; and
- Much more.

Think of each item in the home as a small negative dollar amount. Each one that you bring into the home costs you a bit of enjoyment, so it'd better add value in other ways. Conversely, each item you get rid of is like money in the bank.

This idea in mind, here are a few general tips for lessening clutter in every room of your home:

- **Give stuff away.** Continuously. Remember: it's often much cheaper in the long run to rebuy stuff you gave away a few years back than to deal with the hassle of keeping it all along. Also, every item you donate to (participating) thrift stores is tax deductible for the approximate amount it can sell for—the amount that other similar items sell for in the same store. This means that a coat that is priced at $50 puts $10 in your pocket (if you're in the 20 percent tax bracket)—about as much as you could sell it for at a garage sale. (Note that this rule doesn't apply if you take the standard deduction on your taxes, only if you itemize, and only in the U.S.)
- **Get rid of your furniture.** Also, try not to store furniture you aren't currently using. You can replace anything you end up needing later on with someone else's giveaways—which are often much nicer than your own. Craigslist.org features a "free

stuff" section, and Facebook Buy Nothing groups are also a pretty cool option.

- **When you purchase something new, consider more than the item's functionality.** Picture also how the item will fit the look of your home. Does it match your color scheme, or will it stand out? Is it tacky? (Remember, lots of stuff that looks cute in the store looks that way only because it's part of an entire set, in a showroom that is designed specifically around it.) Is it something that you want to welcome into your experience of life on a daily basis? For example, when deciding which coffee maker to buy, I looked for one that was white (to match my other kitchen appliances) and small (so that I could tuck it away on the shelf next to the coffee rather than leave it out on the counter). I was very happy with that coffee maker for a long as I continued to drink coffee.
- **Store the clutter-making stuff that you can't throw away not on shelves or in closets, but rather in the garage.** Most people don't realize the full value of this invisible room, viewing it as a place to tread as lightly and as infrequently as possible. If you use your garage as storage for everyday items (backup toiletries, chemical cleaners, photographs, etc.), it may get a bit overfull. With excellent organization, though, it will not feel cluttered. Besides, if the garage has to suffer a bit, so be it—you'll still have a Naked House.
- If the garage is tapped out, or you have stuff you

don't want to keep there for reasons of proper preservation, **store it all in a single dedicated, well-organized storage room in the home**—or, better yet, a single closet. It feels better emotionally to keep the clutter sequestered together than to tuck some under this bed, some on that closet shelf, and more under the sink over there.
- If you don't have a garage but do have a backyard, **purchase a moisture-proof shed.** Dehumidifiers can help in these situations, too.

The Naked House is organized; or, A place for everything and everything in its place

As much as I love to expound on the beauty of a clutter-free home, the truth is that there is something that, in terms of home enjoyment, fairly rivals the importance of getting rid of stuff.

And that something is home organization.

But not just any organization—real, thorough, a-place-for-everything-and-everything-in-its-place organization. The kind that drives everyone you live with crazy but that they nevertheless benefit from on a daily basis. The kind where no matter what item is requested, you're able to pinpoint its location immediately within a three-foot radius. The kind that allows for growth, reorganization and expansion. The kind that considers not only ease of item location recall, but ease of access to those items, too.

Simply put, the Naked Home calls for the kind of organization that allows you to rest your head on your pillow at night knowing that every corner of your home is in order.

Sometimes I think that when it comes to keeping a house, my main responsibility is moving objects from here to there. All day long, it happens: clothes to hamper. Remote to DVD player. Hairbrush to basket. Plate to kitchen. Toy to playroom. Fortunately, this process is automatic; because I know the exact place where each of these objects belongs, no time, effort or stress is spent thinking about what to do with them.

That's not to say that it's easy; some days I do experience picking-up-stuff burnout, and on those days I have to take a break before continuing—maybe even take a day off. But awesome organization does reduce the difficulty of cleaning considerably. More important: it makes the "naked" part of the Naked Home possible. 'Cause when a bunch of random things are laying around the house with no dedicated space to call their own, the accumulation of clutter is practically guaranteed.

You may be tempted to skim this section, thinking that you pretty much know where your stuff lives—it's just the keeping of it there that's the problem. But I've been in a number of very clean, well-kept homes that would have been truly naked—if only they were a little better organized.

You probably know what I'm talking about. As you walk through the house for the first time, getting a feel for the place, you see immediately that someone has cared for it well: carpets are vacuumed, garbage cans are empty, dishes are washed, bathroom fixtures sparkle. There are no toys or clothes on the floor, and generally it looks really nice.

But then you look a little closer. (Well, if you're as curious-slash-judgmental as I am you do, anyway.) And that's when you see what the house could easily be, if only everything in it had a place.

On the kitchen counter, appliances crouch protectively, guarding their small squares of space. A set of pots and pans hangs on hooks near the stove, embarrassed by their exposure and awkward pose. Twenty perfect knives flaunt their collective beauty on a magnet on the wall. And an overfull junk drawer stands open, revealing an array of unrelated tools like a glutton loosening his pants.

And then there's the living room. A stunning, carefully decorated place it is—with no box or shelf on which to hide the pile of books, papers or magazines that are currently in use. Several remote controls lie about, and an array of mismatched functional items line the bookshelf in full view. On the coffee table there's a small collection of projects-in-progress, and the TV sits under a pile of movies.

Taken one by one, these are merely slight violations of the Naked Home philosophy. Taken as a whole, though, they change the entire character of the room.

But what's really significant here is how easy the solution is to carry out: matching baskets for the books and projects currently in use, some utility drawers (preferably not in the living room or kitchen) for the tools, and a clear spot in the DVD player cabinet for the movies and remotes. Organizing appliances, knives and pans into cabinets is a bit more time-consuming, but not impossible, and the reward is well worth the effort: the room goes from nice to naked. (Then get rid of the coffee table in the living room and you've really made a good home great.)

Okay, then. Before I leave this topic, I invite you to consider the following list of common household objects and whether or not your home has a dedicated space for each—one that keeps the items largely out of view when not in use:

- The book(s) or magazine(s) you're currently reading;
- The clothes you've worn once but want to wear again before washing (I have a basket set aside for these on top of the dresser);
- The outfit you plan to wear tomorrow;
- Remotes, remotes, remotes (yes, these can be kept out of sight when not in use);
- Food and drinks you want to eat a bit later (I keep all our water glasses in a dedicated spot on the end of one counter till bedtime);
- Keys, wallets and purses; and
- Letters waiting to be mailed.

I will say it again: Create a place for everything—*everything*—and then keep everything in its place. (At least as often as you reasonably can.)

The Naked House is matching; or, How to get a one-story home

One of the subtitles I came up with for this book during a brainstorming session was *How to "Unspeak" Your Home* ... but then I realized it was terrible. However, when discussing the importance of color and style continuity, the metaphor of noise reduction rings true.

Here are some of the words that I found in the thesaurus under *quiet*: still, tranquil, restful, breathable, placid, calm, muted, silent, soft, hushed, low, muffled, mute, reserved, noiseless, secretive, soundless, speechless, and unspeaking.

These words, to me, represent peace (or a big chunk of it, anyway)—the kind of peace I want to bring into my home. And so, the question becomes: how does one make their home quieter? My answer: by matching. Matching colors. Matching styles. Unity, if not uniformity, removes a great deal of distraction.

Which colors to use is, of course, your choice to make. Personally I dislike the color blue, but I can imagine an awesome all blue and white house with various shades of both throughout; done right, it would look like a painting. For me, though, neutral colors like black, tan and brown are the most emotionally satisfying.

Muted colors, for me, dim the noise.

Whichever colors you prefer, here are the four related ideas the Naked House incorporates:

- There are only a few colors (three at most, though black and all shades of white are free);
- The same colors are used throughout the entire home;
- A single base color is used for 80 or 90 percent of the decor; and
- The colors help the inhabitants feel calm.

Why so much rigidity here? Well, it's like this: a truly Naked House—one that feels light, clean and, above all, simple—doesn't distract the inhabitants with lots of color noise, or with color separations in each room. Instead, it allows people to walk throughout the home and experience (in a subconscious way, of course) the same sense of harmony in one room that they felt in the last—no jarring transitions or out-of-context ideas. The feeling of unity, of oneness they get—well, you may even think of it as spiritual.

Your house has a soul, and it has a story to tell—and it's best if that story makes sense.

Now, there's more to matching than color, of course: there's also matching styles and such. This, admittedly, is a bit more difficult and requires some planning in advance. However, if every time you shop for the home you keep the principle of matching in mind, eventually the small changes will make a difference—one that you will certainly appreciate.

Here are a few ideas to implement as you are able:

- **Choose a single theme or era** to represent—one that matches the basic personality of your home already. (Mine is the 1950's.)
- **Try not to go overboard on your theme.** Instead, **buy mostly plain stuff** so it doesn't date out and so you can easily replace it with look-alikes later on.
- **Whenever possible, avoid buying just one set of anything.** Buy several at least, so that you can use the same product throughout the entire home and for a long time to come. (This tip

particularly applies to: dishes, towels, bedding, laundry baskets, storage baskets and boxes, and lamps. I regret not buying more of my lightweight, baby-safe, high-quality bedroom lamps, which at the time I thought were overpriced, for the kids' room and office, too.)

- **Try not to mix woods.** Choose a stain hue and stick with it.
- **Reconsider your home's hardware.** Make it a goal to little by little replace all the doorknobs, cabinet handles, sink fixtures, towel racks—even the fireplace grate and the vent covers—with a single simple color and style. One of my first home improvement projects in my new home was to replace all the outlet covers, light switch covers, and bathroom cabinet knobs with polished brass. (My husband fights me on this, though, saying plastic is safer for electrical stuff. Whatever!)
- As stated before, **choose a single base color and buy everything (or nearly everything) in that color.**

Remember: your home is a work of art. So make sure it's a single, unified work—not a big, eclectic, strange collection.

The Naked House is clean ... or, at the very least, easily cleaned

I remember a time not too long ago when I truly and honestly loved to clean. Those were my pre-kids days, of course, when cleaning actually provided me with a convenient excuse to get out from behind my computer screen or book and do something that felt immediately productive. I would straighten pillows and clear off tables and wipe counters. I would wash every dish in the sink nearly every day. For a period of about four years, I even took real pleasure in cooking.

Alas, these days are no longer—a time for everything and a season to every purpose under heaven, as they say. Now I spend every free minute I have trying to get behind the computer, the notebook, or the book (which is also, of course, fine with me).

The point is this: my house is not perfectly clean all the time—and I don't expect yours to be, either. When I say that the fourth principle of the Naked House is that it's clean, here is what I'm trying to convey: it is easy to clean. Since there is a place for everything, the before-bed routine is a simple matter of unthinkingly returning objects to their proper resting places (rather than trying to reorganize them at the same time), wiping the few surfaces you own and maybe emptying the dishwasher or folding some clothes. Having a whole lot less stuff overall supports this goal too, of course: there's less stuff to put away, less stuff to work around and less stuff to wipe down or dust. As you'll see later on in this book, cleaning most of my rooms is a simple matter of picking the clothes or toys off the floor and vacuuming. (Of course, this isn't true of the kitchen, but we'll get to that later on.)

And here's something else you should know: even when the Naked House isn't clean, it feels okay. Most of the time, there are some dishes in my kitchen sink. Most of the time, there are some toys strewn around my family room floor. A lot of the time, there's toothpaste residue in my bathroom sink, and I normally don't make the bed. (My living room is nearly always perfect, but that's just my way of satisfying my obsessive-compulsive tendencies in a not-so-all-consuming manner.)

And yet, my house usually feels under control.

And so, here is what I say about cleaning the house: if it comes down to a choice between cleaning and organizing, choose organizing. Then just do what cleaning you can.

When remodeling, consider easy-to-clean fixtures, moldings and more

A final note on cleanliness: Over time, I have discovered that appliances, cabinetry, window frames, lights and other house fixtures are rarely as easy to clean as they should be. Consider the shape of the standard toilet: round sides, hard-to-reach curves underneath. Worse, most toilets are not placed flush against the back wall, and this is where dust and—well, other matter—collects. If you are in the process of renovation or are considering renovating in the future, consider choosing styles that use simple, clean lines. I sometimes tell my husband that if I had a square toilet (they do exist, by the way, and they're nice-looking), I would save approximately a month of cleaning time over the course of my life. This is an estimate, of course, and likely a terrible one. But I hate cleaning the toilet. Any time saved cleaning it would be worth making the change.

A few other trouble spots to consider when remodeling: the spaces between the fridge and the counter and between the stove and the counter (some stove models can be built in, nixing this problem; otherwise, consider using some kind of trim to bridge the gap if possible); tiny edging, as on floor trim, door trim, window trim or cabinets (smoother styles are available and won't attract grime that you'll have to scrape out once a year); simple, smooth lights without any metal decoration. If you're a very busy person and you're brave enough to put duct tape around your stove, fridge and wash/dry machines, go for it. With my sincere congratulations. (The stuff that lives beneath those machines is the worst kind of stuff.) I will admit that I used clear packing tape to seal the drawer underneath my stove closed. It's a grime trap.

Curtains are easier to clean than blinds by far. Dark carpet is cool-looking and you're not constantly spraying and scrubbing. Tile is one of the worst choices you can make in terms of cleanliness. Glossy paint is also better than flat (the shiny surface resists marks much better).

The Naked Home is quality; Or, Invest in the home—not so much the stuff in it

Though it is admittedly the least important aspect of the Naked House, it's a principle worth expounding on nonetheless: The Naked House is of high quality.

Now, while price is often a preventative factor in this matter, I do not mean to convince you to choose only the most expensive items for your home, or that spending more money is always necessary. When I say "quality," what I mean is that each and every item in the home is chosen with great care and serious attention to its relative merits. Paint samples are pored over, and walls are repainted if the first shade isn't quite right. Kitchen appliances are carefully considered and selected. Gifts are sometimes (often?) given again. In short: Everything that becomes a permanent or semi-permanent part of the atmosphere of your home earns it's right to be there by fulfilling all or most of the following requirements:

- It is the appropriate color;
- It is truly useful;
- It is not cheap-looking, tacky or otherwise distracting; and
- It makes you feel proud to own it.

Of course, these ideas don't apply just to the objects in your home; they apply to an even greater degree to the design decisions you make. In my experience, good flooring—plush, unstained carpet or professionally finished hardwood floors—and high-end paint can together make up 90 percent of the home's decor.

Let's take a moment to consider that statement. Imagine your home exactly as it is now, but with absolutely no furnishing at all, as if you hadn't yet moved in. Now imagine repainting it in any color or colors you choose, buffing the hardwood floors to a shine and getting all new carpet. Wouldn't "decorating" the home then seem mostly unnecessary—something that would subtract from rather than adding to the simple, beautiful effect you just created?

Eventually, when the time and bank account balance is right, you can add to these basics excellent, indirect and dimmable lighting and a number of other quality improvements you've no doubt thought of yourself. For now, though, I recommend that you invest in the walls and floors if you can, then give great care and attention to the items you layer over that beautiful base.

A few additional thoughts on the subject before I move on:

- **When planning a move, consider buying a smaller home in a better location with a better floor plan rather than a larger home that's a bit further out or that you don't love walking into.** Quality relates not just to durability, but also to lifestyle enjoyment. Remember: the Naked Home is much bigger than it at first seems to be.
- As I mentioned before, **buy plain, durable items that don't date out.** High-quality is not a synonym for fancy. If you like fancy or embellished objects, buy just a few and keep the rest plain; this way you can easily change styles later on.
- **If you don't have the money to redecorate, your house can still be impressive.** A good friend of mine who (happily) lives under the poverty level has a house I consider to be brimming with potential—one I could enjoy without spending a dime. You'd be surprised how beautiful a comfy old couch and a scuffed floor can look, when the space around them is bare, well-organized and clean.

And so, the Naked House is bare. It is organized, and it is clean and high-quality. Above all else, though, the Naked House is a place in which you feel good. You have everything you need. You feel comfortable with the way it looks. You know where everything is. You don't feel suffocated.

It's a place where you can truly relax.

If you can say that about your home, you can ignore every tip in this book and still be aligned with its message.

Now we turn to our tour of the Naked Home, starting with its pride and joy: the living room.

Naked Interview
Mary Potter Kenyon: "I Shed Tears Through the Process"

Mary Potter Kenyon is a grief counselor and the author of seven books, including Refined By Fire: A Journey of Grief and Grace *and* Called to Be Creative. *She lives in Dubuque, Iowa. For more information, see MaryPotterKenyon.com.*

Mollie: Have you ever significantly reorganized and decluttered your home? What led to the decision and what did you change?

Mary: In April 2018, I was offered my dream job an hour from where I lived. I made the decision to sell the four-bedroom, two-story house where my husband David and I had raised the last four of our eight children. David had died in 2012 and my seventh child was poised to leave the nest, leaving me with one daughter and a huge house. Not only did I need to declutter in order to sell my house, the house I purchased in my new town was 760 square feet. I had to do some serious purging, with less than two months to do it.

I began by deciding which furniture could come with me, and my heart sank when I realized my four bookshelves, my huge solid oak desk and my mother's kitchen table would not fit. The owner of the house I was buying agreed to leave a folding IKEA table in the kitchen, the only kind of table that worked. Two living room chairs would need to be sold. A beautiful closed cabinet that was filled with office supplies and photo albums. A kitchen shelf. The one thing I knew had to come with me was a shaker-style cabinet I'd inherited from my mother, but it would need to be emptied of some of her things to make room for the single shelf of books I would keep.

I went through closets of clothing. As I pulled things off hangers, I priced those I thought would sell. I even had a box of my husband's shirts stashed away, which my sister Joan agreed to take off my hands and make into Christmas stockings for my children. I wasn't just dealing with stuff, I was dealing with memories, and **I shed tears through the process.** I went through thousands of books. The first two boxes sold for $150 at a bookstore, alleviating the distress a little. By the time I held my first garage sale, I'd whittled down my possessions drastically. The most daunting task, though, was the paper: a file cabinet and a trunk filled with letters, college papers, photos, and even scrapbooks from high school. I handed my son a bag filled with twenty day books (daily diaries) to burn because I couldn't bear to dispose of them myself.

After two garage sales, several trips to a thrift store, and even filling my front lawn with items I advertised for free on a local online giveaway board, I ended up with less than half my original possessions. By then, it felt freeing to have dealt with years of accumulated clutter—to have made decisions about which things meant the most and gave me pleasure and joy when I looked at them. I would come to regret only the loss of the desk and the day books.

While I no longer have a separate office, I do have my own space, a back room that spans the entire width of the house and serves as both bedroom and office. Everything in it was consciously chosen to survive the Great Purge of 2018. The bedroom portion is sparse: an end table and a twin bed topped with a mockingbird quilt that matches the curtains. Outside of a washer and dryer in the opposite far corner, the rest of the large room is designed around the comfy brown recliner my children gave me for Christmas. When I sit in it to write or read, I'm surrounded by things that bring a smile to my face.

There is the Shaker-style cabinet I inherited from my mother, filled with things I treasure: my collection of autographed books, a hand-blown glass turtle my son Michael made, a toy sheep from my childhood, and bricks my daughter Rachel painted to look like the covers of my books. My grandmother's trunk is topped by one of Mom's quilts and her hand-carved Saint Michael statue, his sword upraised in regal glory.

Walls are adorned with paintings by my mother and daughter Emily, along with photographs taken by my son Dan, one framed and another on canvas. A rustic wooden rack is attached to one wall, the wire baskets holding stationery and greeting cards. Wooden letters with the cover designs of my six books on another wall spell the word "writer," handmade by my daughter Elizabeth. Finally, there's a book-themed lamp atop an end table Katie painted to look like book spines. **I love my smaller space.**

Mollie: What are your most prized beliefs regarding the minimalist lifestyle—the ideas you want most to spread?

Mary: We can survive, and even thrive, with less stuff. It can be very freeing to let go of things that just take up space. Living in clutter causes a lot of stress and anxiety, whether we are aware of it or not. Living in a smaller space means I have to be careful what I bring into the house. I find I can't write amid clutter. When my space is a mess, my thoughts are a mess, too.

Mollie: Can you share a few very specific tips for cleaning, organizing and simplifying a home (and maybe a life, too)?

Mary: If you can, **take your time in choosing what you will get rid of.** I had less than two months, and really had to rush the process, resulting in a couple of rash decisions I now regret. Also, unless your house is full of actual garbage, please don't throw things away in an attempt to rid your house of clutter. I always cringe when I watch reality shows where someone goes into a hoarder's house and starts throwing things away, even bags of new clothing or toys. It's true: your discards are someone else's treasure. Donate to charity. Hold a garage sale. Making money off your decluttering makes the process a little less painful.

Make an art project around some of the little mementos you have hidden away in boxes and drawers. I had my mother's newspaper clippings about her art, her holy medals, several rosaries, some handwritten notes, a pencil she used to draw with. I wasn't enjoying those things hidden away in a drawer, but I love the mixed media project I created out of those things, a visual reminder of my beloved mother. I'm making one with some mementos from my husband's life next.

2

THE NAKED LIVING ROOM

THE NAKED LIVING Room is bare

Often, when I ponder the concept of the Naked House, a certain image comes to mind. It is the image of my living room. Not as it is now, though; instead, it's the image of my living room the first time that I saw it.

The house was shown unfurnished, and I will never forget the moment I followed the real estate agent through the front door. I knew immediately that this was my house. Our house: the one David, myself and the baby inside me would share. Simply put, I loved everything about it.

As I meandered through the bare rooms one by one, I made myself a promise: whatever I brought into this fresh new space would only make it better. The spirit of these clean, off-white walls and furniture-free floor spaces wouldn't be entirely lost during the large scale transfer of goods that would have to happen.

I would make the space livable, but I would not ruin its best quality: the natural beauty that lies underneath the layers of clothing we'd add to make it presentable. I would dress my home simply. That was my intention, and for the most part, I've honored it.

My living room isn't the room in my house that has the least amount of furniture—the family room has only a single small shelf—no sitting furniture—and the small bedroom has only a bed. And yet, this room to me is the better representation of the Naked Home's essence because it lacks the single greatest obstacle to nakedness. And that obstacle is of course what we call clutter.

My family room has it; though we sit on a blanket or bean bags on the floor, that floor is often strewn with toys. My bedroom has it; there are visible clothes in the hamper at all times, as well as a book or two by the bed. But the living room is the soul of the house, the place that most lives up to the ideal. Here, there are no pictures on the wall and only a single one on the shelf. There are no end tables to collect water glasses or magazines, and no coffee table to do the same. Every object in the room is placed exactly where I want it to be—and each one serves a specific purpose.

Here is a list of everything that's visible in this (admittedly not so big) space:

- Two matching black leather couches;
- A matching black leather chair;
- Three matching black leather foot rests;
- A TV;
- A small TV stand;
- A fireplace with a metal cover;
- One built-in wall shelf;
- Two matching vases;

- One picture;
- One candle;
- Two matching decorative pillows;
- A decorative throw blanket; and
- Lightweight curtains.

And here are just some of the items commonly found in living rooms that I think often—maybe even usually—need not be there:

- Lamps;
- Lamp tables/end tables;
- Fireplace pokers (we use only one, and it stays in the garage);
- Knickknacks;
- Dishes;
- Papers and mail;
- Books;
- Toys;
- Wall hangings (no, not even one, particularly if you have nice big windows);
- Blankets and throws, especially those that don't match;
- Shoes and slippers;
- Coats;
- Coat racks;
- Coffee tables;
- Shelves, drawers or cabinets;
- CDs and DVDs (these can be hidden or, if too numerous, kept in the office or garage);
- TVs and related equipment, if you have a room for them somewhere else;
- Music players (I keep ours on top of our fridge,

well out of sight);
- Home entertainment centers (use a small TV stand instead if you need one);
- Furniture that's purely decorative, such as china closets, uncomfortable antique chairs and benches, hope chests and the like;
- Ornate furniture and fixtures, unless used sparingly;
- Heavy or heavy-feeling curtains (unless the style and size of your home can handle them without seeming overwhelmed);
- Other practical daily items that rightfully belong in other rooms.

In addition, some items, such as the TV remote or the movie we're going to watch later, can be hidden out of view (in this case, inside the TV stand).

The good news for people who love pretty things: the living room is still the best place to put them. I suggest limiting these to one or two—not more than three—so their beauty can be truly appreciated.

The Naked Living Room is clean; or, When there's a party, drag the mess to the kitchen

Unlike most of the other rooms in the Naked House, the living room need not be especially well-organized; after all, there isn't much in there. No drawers. No desks. No shelves, if you can help it. The living room simply isn't used for storage. And because the Naked Home principle of good organization is sort of a given here, the principle of cleanliness is also quite easily followed.

THE NAKED HOUSE

Unlike the kitchen, bedroom, playroom/family room, bathroom and office, the living room doesn't compel time-consuming cleaning processes like dish washing, clothes laundering, grout maintenance or counter wiping. Even if you spend a lot of time here working on projects, watching TV and the like, at the end of the evening everything can be removed to another location. When you return to it in the morning, the room is whole again. It is its carefully planned, cherished self.

Here are the tasks I undertake in my living room after a typical dinner-and-movie evening:

- I clear the dining room table and wipe it down. I push in the chairs.
- I sweep the floor or run the Rumba.
- I put our movie back into the case and put it, along with the remotes, into the TV stand.
- I put away the blanket, if we used one.
- I push our foot rests back into position.

On a recent morning after a dinner party at my home my friend Julie came by to drop off a container.

"Your house is always so clean!" she told me, surprised. "I'd never know there was a party here last night!"

She didn't see the disaster in the kitchen. But I didn't feel the need to mention it. Someday, she'll learn the truth.

The Naked Living Room is quality; or, Splurge on the paint, not the couch

I'll discuss my love of the Naked Home principle of matching more later, and its importance to the Naked Living Room is great. But the Naked House idea that I believe the living room has the best chance of showcasing is that of quality.

Newly refinished hardwood floors. Designer paint. Great lighting (which, by the way, is exceedingly difficult to find). A few art pieces and a clean couch (or a clean couch cover on an old couch). None of these things are cheap, but some investments are worth it.

Given the choice between buying a new set of furniture of good flooring and paint, choose the flooring and paint every time. Improve the house, not the stuff that sits inside the house. If you deeply desire new furniture, find some excellent bargains online and rent a truck. When people see your home, it's likely that subconsciously, they will base their beauty assessments on the home itself, not on the scratched table that you don't want to replace until your kids are old enough not to bang their forks on it. A friend of mine moved into a two-million-plus dollar home and brought her old, battered kitchen table with it. I didn't notice. I sat in one of the chairs and the arm rest broke off. I laughed. It didn't matter. Her house was amazing, and I respected her decision to invest in what was more permanent.

Our couch set has been with my husband for fifteen years, and one of the cushions is terribly torn. Our (admittedly ugly) dining room table and chairs are even older—hand-me-downs of a rather cheap variety. No one minds. The house is uncluttered. I threw some old sheets over the chairs so they'd blend in, and sometimes I use a tablecloth.

THE NAKED HOUSE

In short, my advice on increasing the quality of the living room (and that of any other room in the home): Splurge on professionally redone floors and good paint; this might be all the decor you will need.

I maintain that the main reason this room looks so nice is the lack of clutter, but the warm paint and newly refinished hardwood floor are elements very nearly as significant.

Naked Interview
Nick D'Urso: "My Car Is My Home and the World is My Bedroom"

Nick is a freewheeling AirBnB rental owner. He teaches people how to make their money work for them (rather than the other way around) at NickDurso.com.

Mollie: Have you ever significantly minimized your possessions and simplified your life? Tell me the story.

In July 2019 I left my corporate job back home in Brooklyn, New York. I bought a car in Phoenix, Arizona to drive to Argentina. I pretty much left everything I owned except a few clothes, my laptop, a camera, and a drone. I built a bed in the back of the car and I have been living on the road ever since, camping at some of the most beautiful places in Mexico. I'm about to enter Belize.

My car is my home and the world is my bedroom.

Mollie: What did you buy along the way? Do you have good camping equipment?

Nick: I haven't bought much. I bought a new suspension for the car and two front lower control arms. The car is old and I was worried about the rust and being stuck in a country with no parts if something happened. Other than that, I bought a cooler, folding chairs, and a BBQ. At some point I'll have to buy winter clothes when I reach Argentina but I'll tackle that when I get there. I also bought a new phone using Google Fi because it works in over 200 countries on their unlimited plan.

Mollie: How long do you plan to travel and what will you do after that?

Nick: Everyone asks me this question. Truthfully I'm planning this trip to find a place where I can build another AirBNB property close to the water so I can run scuba diving excursions. I don't have a time limit. My goal is to travel around the entire world and it's taken me 6 months to do all of Mexico. I promised my mom and dad I would spend Christmas with them in 2020. But other than that I don't have a time limit.

Mollie: What led to this drastic change?

Nick: The thing that led me to this decision was being caught up in the humdrum of everyday corporate life living in New York City. I personally couldn't take going to work every day to make money to spend at a bar on the weekends with friends, over and over again. I wanted to get more out of life.

Mollie: What do you want to get out of life?

Nick: I would like to teach people that money isn't everything. It's a vehicle to get you to where you want to be. We're all taught that we need to go to school and get a job that pays well. Everyone wants a raise and to earn more money. But the truth is that you most likely make enough money and that money can actually make you more money but your habits prevent that. People look at my Instagram and ask me how I do this. I tell them I drive a '98 Chevy Blazer with a bed in it. You don't need a lot of money to do what I'm doing; you just need to change your habits. And that's the mark I want to leave. Money is great, but you don't need to exchange time to earn more. Other than that I would say I just want to be happy and meet amazing people all around the world.

Mollie: What are your most prized beliefs regarding minimalist lifestyle—the ideas you most want to spread?

Nick: My most prized beliefs behind my minimalist lifestyle change is that it doesn't matter what anyone thinks about you. I want to spread that to everyone around. With social media nowadays, most people seem to be in competition with people they don't even know.

Mollie: Tell me more about what you mean.

Nick: I believe that there are a lot of fake things in our world. I saw it in my corporate job. I would get awarded for things that looked really great but in all reality I didn't do anything. Social media plays a part in this. I could have posted a picture of me holding a trophy from work then pictures of me at a huge waterfall in Mexico and paint the picture that I'm killing it at work and I earn tons of money to travel the world. Then other people think in order to be happy they need a high-paying job. If you truly stop worrying about what other people have and think about you, then you won't make this ever-ending bubble of competition for yourself and you can be happy.

Mollie: Can you share a few very specific tips for living more simply?

Nick: Automating your life through leveraging your hard-earned money is key. You don't need much to be happy. One huge tip I would love to share is to put your head down and work for ten years—and work hard! There's no shortcut, but compounding interest investments are your friend. Save your money to purchase yourself some sort of asset, like a house, to fund your life. Don't trade your time for money. It's difficult but it's important to alter your habits to achieve a minimalist lifestyle filled with free time doing the things you want and love.

**Naked Interview
Tara Skubella: "Living in an Off-grid Tiny Home Is Extremely Important to Me"**

Tara Skubella teaches tantra and conducts tantra ceremonies. See nakedearthtantra.com.

Mollie: Tell me about your minimalist lifestyle.

Tara: My partner and I are minimalists who live in a tiny home (a converted fifth-wheel) nearly off-grid on the side of a mountain. We've been here for three years and love it. We've condensed so much of our lives to make this our truth. Not only are we tiny house minimalists, but we don't have running potable water and heat with wood.

Mollie: What was your decluttering and simplifying process like?

Tara: My first decluttering process happened while I was living in a 1400 square foot house. I donated, gifted or threw away 365 things in my home that I no longer needed. These items ranged from old cleaning products and makeup to pairs of earrings to clothing to a piece of furniture to kitchen supplies and books. It's amazing how fast you can rid of items no longer used.

This became a ritual I continue to do about every other year, even while living in a tiny home. Most of the items I release these days are small things like pens or pencils, makeup, notebooks, accessories, old food and clothing items. It feels good to have a fresh start every now and then. Releasing 365 things clears the mind and gives us one less object to worry or think about each day for a year.

Mollie: What are your most prized beliefs regarding minimalist lifestyle? What ideas you want to spread?

Tara: Living a minimalist, off-grid, tiny-home life is extremely important to me. I enjoy being immersed in Mother Nature. I depend on snow for water to do my dishes and to boil water for tea. I depend on dead standing wood to heat our tiny home during the harsh 9,000-foot winter months. Living with Mother Earth instead of carving space into her creates a wealth of gratitude each day. Even living the primitive way I do is still very abundant, as I've experienced harsh survival situations in the past. Coming home to a cozy, safe space warms my heart.

I also believe living with less helps me with my ADHD. Since my mind is cluttered most of the time, living in a space with less to clean and to worry about simplifies my life even more. Living with less is also a mindful life choice and practice. Consciously choosing what we can live without opens the spirit to reconnect with intuitive choices about what we truly need in order to survive. Otherwise, instead of being more mindful of tasks we look for an easy way out. Thinking this way sometimes isn't a big deal; however, the more we develop an attachment to objects for meeting our needs, the more we look for answers outside instead of within.

Mollie: Can you share a few very specific tips for cleaning, organizing and simplifying a home?

Tara: Yes. First, if you haven't used something in a little over a year, you really don't need it so get rid of it.

Second, if you bring a non-perishable item into the house, release something else as an exchange. For example, if you buy a new pair of socks, donate or gift a pair that has never really fit right. If you receive a fancy new air-vacuumed mug for your birthday, donate the plastic one that doesn't keep coffee warm as long as your new one.

Also, remember that linens and towels can add up quickly. We only need one to two sets of sheets per bed and one to two bath towels per person. Depending on the family size, three or four kitchen towels is plenty. People often accumulate too many linens because we don't like to do the laundry. This accumulation also happens with clothing. The more we are able to be mindful with laundry, the less we actually need on hand.

My final tip is to rent a storage unit. Seriously. If you are uncertain about releasing a number of items, rent a storage unit and place those items in it, then see how often you return to use them. For the items you truly need, you'll be willing to drive to the unit, use it and drive it back. If items stay unused for several months or they aren't worth the rental fee, then you'll learn that those unused items aren't worth the money and effort to keep around.

3

THE NAKED KITCHEN

THE NAKED KITCHEN is matching

When I was growing up my mother didn't give much thought to the way her kitchen looked. The living room—sure, that was always picked up and vacuumed. The family room was kept clean and functional, too.

But the kitchen was just a place to store the food.

The cabinets, especially, were a mess. Though Mom never gave in to the kind of appliance proliferation that is so common today, it wasn't because she was purposely trying to stay more organized; she just didn't have the extra money.

Following, a brief tour of the kitchen cabinets of my childhood home. (Oh, and just for the record: my mom's house is totally minimalist now.)

- **Under the bar (north side):** A collection of beautiful, delicate china so large, varied and crammed, we could hardly ever locate two teacups that were the same. And more papers.

- **Under the bar (south side):** Papers. Stacks and stacks of papers, plus a great assortment of other non-kitchen items: pens, art supplies, toys, books and more, all mixed up together on the shelves.
- **Over the counter (east side):** Mismatched plates, glasses, bowls and mugs, especially—oh, especially!—the mugs. I think I must have been truly traumatized as a child by having to choose between the light pink "Happy Mother's Day" cup that came beautifully wrapped and filled with chocolates one year, or one of the chipped Christmas mugs that (to her very great delight) Mom won at a white elephant gift exchange. And so, one of the first things I bought for our new house—even before moving in, actually—was a set of matching glasses and mugs—so many of them I still have an overflow section in the back of one cabinet. (They are beautiful.)
- **Corner cabinet (east side):** The spice rack. Need I say more?
- **Corner cabinet (west side):** Assorted pantry items small enough to fit on a turntable-type rack, canned goods and vitamins.
- **Over the counter (west side):** Larger pantry items.
- **Under the stove and under the counters:** Appliances and cookware that rarely made an appearance on the same shelf twice in a row, and tons of empty sour cream, yogurt and cottage cheese cartons of all different sizes to use on the go (don't even bother trying to find a matching lid).

Again, these made a deep impression on me; my initial purchase of twenty-eight rectangle Pyrex containers, all of exactly the same size and shape, was sent straight to my new house before we even moved in. This set was eventually joined by forty-two more of the same, and today they line an entire cabinet shelf, an entire refrigerator shelf and two or three separate shelves in our freezers. I also bought lunchboxes of the same dimensions that hold exactly three rectangle Pyrexes with enough extra room at the top for a piece of fruit.

And so, that is a glimpse into my childhood kitchen, with a bit of psychology mixed in, too. (You're welcome.)

Here's the thing: Lots of people can't afford to buy hundreds of perfectly matching containers for their various culinary needs. I get that—really, I do. However, there are also a whole lot of people that find a set they like and can afford, then don't buy enough of that set to be able to get rid of the old set entirely. Then they get a few gifts or souvenirs that also don't match, and before you know it their cabinets are no longer visually appealing (or space efficient).

- You might be thinking that having matching dishes isn't exactly your priority in life. And so, if you're truly unable to afford new stuff right now, my advice is that you pare it down as much as you can (at the very least get rid of the mismatched china you never use, no matter how "valuable" you think it is). Then, when you do eventually decide to replace a few things, keep these simple guidelines in mind:

- **Buy everything in the plainest possible style,** particularly tall glasses which tend to break most often. If you buy clear pint glasses in the style used by most bars and restaurants, you'll never have to replace a whole set at once.
- **Don't get the expensive stuff.** High-end dishes will almost certainly date out. My choice: Correll bowls and plates in plain white. They are thin and lightweight (qualities that with daily use turn out to be even more awesome than you think they will be), very durable and go with any decor. And the manufacturer hasn't changed the size or shape in years and years.
- **Copy my Pyrex purchase.** After an afternoon comparison shopping online, I bought the Pyrex® Simply Store® 3-cup Rectangular Dish. Unlike round containers they fit perfectly in fridge, freezer and cabinet corners, and they hold more food than round ones, too. They're also the perfect size for dinner or lunch. If you think you can't live without the larger containers, try it first. Whole-family meals can easily be divided up among several containers, and so can potluck contributions. (Remember: The Naked House isn't about not having stuff; it's about only having the stuff that serves you well.)
- **No matter which to-go container brand you decide on, try not to be tempted by the lower price of the multi-piece set.** Instead, choose a single size and shape, and buy more of that one piece than you think you'll ever need. As I mentioned before, this saves tons of

THE NAKED HOUSE

space in your cabinets, fridge and dishwasher—but it's also a whole lot easier to find the matching lid.

- **When updating, use only plain tile of a single color, with no distracting patterns of any kind.**
- **Decide on a single towel color and buy potholders, too, to match.**
- Particularly if you have children, **consider replacing your silverware drawer with a silverware bucket that you keep in a cabinet.** This way, you can easily carry it to and from the dining room table.
- **Buy all appliances—large and small—in the same color.** This will usually be stainless steel or white. Doing so, of course, gives a cleaner, more uniform look to your kitchen. Personally, I'm proud to have all white appliances since in my humble opinion, stainless steel looks out of place in a 1950's style home. (Plus, I saved a bunch of money when replacing them.)
- **Bonus points are given for matching spatula sets, knife sets, pots and pans, etc.,** even though these are kept out of sight.

MOLLIE PLAYER

> My Pyrex collection makes me feel proud, as well as embarrassed by how proud I feel. I can't tell you how often we empty out this cabinet, stocking our refrigerator and extra freezer with pre-prepared meals ... but it's often.

THE NAKED HOUSE

My inexpensive Correll dishes fit nicely on a single small shelf—and stack well in the dishwasher, too.

MOLLIE PLAYER

THE NAKED HOUSE

Due to the lack of counter top clutter, when my kitchen is clean, it actually looks it. I don't love the tile counter tops or the walnut cabinets (come to think of it, the floor is pretty ugly, too), but things like that aren't too bothersome when a room is well-kept.

Naked Interview
Pablo Solomon:"Voids Can Give Meaning and Emphasis to Chosen Elements"

Pablo and Beverly Solomon have been minimalist designers for over forty years. Their work has been featured in over forty books as well as numerous magazines and newspapers; on TV and film; and on the radio. You can see examples of their fashion and home designs at PabloSolomon.com and BeverlySolomon.com.

Mollie: What is the essence of your minimalist design philosophy?

Pablo: You have so often heard it said that the core of minimalism is the concept of "less is more". We would modify that a bit and say that **putting quality over quantity is also minimalism.** Minimalism is also the recognition that simplifying your life and achieving a harmonious balance between things and experiences, between your comfort and respecting nature, between activity and rest, etc. are also goals. **Minimalism strives to be a physical representation of a serene, uncluttered mind that lives in harmony with nature.**

Mollie: That's an interesting idea. What does minimalism have in common with living in harmony with nature?

Pablo: Beverly is part Native American. One of her core beliefs that we try to follow is that we are just passing through this life and should leave the smallest negative marks behind—that we respect nature by using only what we need and protecting the rest. Minimalism design not only tries to blend the architecture into the setting, but to do the least amount of damage in the process. The concept of your home blending into the setting is representative of your being part of nature, not at odds with nature.

Mollie: Can you share a few specific tips for living a successful minimalist lifestyle?

Pablo: It really begins with choosing to live in harmony with nature and to create a setting for yourself that puts you at peace. Keep the things that you cherish, that bring you happy memories, that make your life more pleasant. Eliminate those elements that just fill space for the sake of filling space. **Learn to embrace the concept that voids can give meaning and emphasis to chosen elements.** And it is okay to be as minimal or non-minimal as makes you comfortable.

Mollie: How do voids help give meaning? Can you give me an example of how you would use a void in an interior or exterior home design?

Pablo: The most simple example would be a wall. Having one valued painting is emphasized by the blank space around it. Were the wall to have as many paintings as you can cram on that wall, no one painting would have much impact.

Mollie: Any other thoughts?

Pablo: Like so many truths in life, the journey is often more important than the destination. Just considering the mindset of minimalism and taking the first steps in simplifying your life and calming your mind are worth it. Just let go of one thing today. Tomorrow is another day.

4

THE NAKED FAMILY ROOM

THE NAKED FAMILY Room is organized and bare

When Dave and I bought our current home, we didn't have any children. We loved everything about the house—the size, the entryway, the layout, the big yard. However, behind the beautiful living room was another much smaller room, and I found myself wondering what I'd ever use it for. A meditation room? A reading room? A library? Then I made one of the luckiest purchases of my life—thick, high-quality carpet in dark brown, discovered by chance after already having paid a deposit on a much cheaper, thinner style—and suddenly the room just made sense. *It's a play room*, I realized. *A place to wrestle and read, to spread out our toys—to do anything you'd want to do on a floor.* A few years and about a thousand toys later, I laugh at myself for wondering if I'd ever use this wonderful, special room.

There's something about sitting on the floor that's just fun. That's what I think, and apparently I'm not the only one: Steve Jobs (famous as much for his simple design aesthetic as his technical accomplishments, as you know) reportedly eschewed the use of couches in his home for many years. For comfort, we use bean bags and reading pillows, those pillows that come with arms that you put against the wall. (My husband dubbed them "chillows," as in, "pillows for chillin'.") We can rearrange the "furniture" anytime, making room for chasing, dancing and forts, and our square-footage-challenged family room never seems to me all that small.

I don't have to remind you of the joys of the family room, though, I'm sure. Even if you just use it to watch TV and relax, it's a place in which you always feel comfortable. Because of that, perfect tidiness probably won't be your priority here. However, as stated about other rooms with clutter control issues, if you adhere to the guidelines of the Naked Family Room, even the messy times won't overwhelm.

Not that this solution is easy to carry out. In my experience, the family room (or the living room/family room if there's just one) is the home's central magnet of clutter.

There are good reasons for this, of course. You read here, so why not have a bookshelf? You watch movies here, so obviously this is the place to store your collection. You eat here, so cups and plates are commonly found.

And then, of course, there are the toys.

Much of this mess is excusable; however, that doesn't mean that all of it is. A bunch of things frequently end up in the family room for reasons other than usefulness and convenience.

They are they because there's nowhere else for them to go.

This is a sadness. Extra lamp tables, barely-used box fans, and the antique rocking chair bought at a garage sale one year ... larger items like these are only the beginning. Even more insidious is the small stuff: stacks of paper. A can with assorted pencils and pens. Disorganized junk drawers. Light bulbs, cleaning supplies, batteries, last week's knitting project, a pair of scissors. With no other set-aside home base for these necessary little things they'll end up on the coffee table every time.

My solution: a pantry or office shelves or both. If your home comes equipped with neither, an inexpensive cabinet insert can be placed in a hall closet.

And that is where all the extras will go.

In my home, we have a pantry as well as an office. One pantry wall holds food items, while the other has a set of five drawers that we call our utility drawers. Here's what's in them:

- **The top drawer:** Scissors, writing tools, tape, glue, and the like, as well as one of each type of screwdriver.
- **The second drawer:** Batteries, flashlights and candles.
- **The third drawer:** Vacuum bags, plastic gloves and other non-liquid cleaning-related items.
- **The bottom drawer:** Miscellaneous stuff, making it the only true junk drawer of the house. Here, items are separated in plastic bags by type. The bags are home to spare keys, twist ties, fabric scraps, and more.

All other office supplies, like envelopes and paper, books, computer paraphernalia, current paperwork and a few other things, are in the office. Photos are kept on the computer and the few photo albums that haven't been digitized live in a single box in the garage.

When you really sit down and think about it, you may be surprised at how few items are truly "at home" in the family room; in ours, there are just bean bags, pillows, toys, diapers and clothes (our baby changing station is on the family room floor) and a low two-drawer cabinet with books.

Here are some additional tips for an awesome, Feng Shui-worthy family room:

- **Keep the walls bare, free of wall hangings of any kind.** Not only do they bring the walls in closer, they lose their freshness quickly, becoming tiresome to look at.
- **When looking for a new home, consider choosing a separate living room and family room over a larger single front room.** It's also preferable to see only the living room from the front entrance of the home, not the family room.
- **Consider not using bright paint in an older home.** Unless you've remodeled down to the last door handle (and that includes the doors themselves), bold, bright colors bring out the imperfections in the home: cracked drywall, old vent covers, old-fashioned wall and window trim, etc.
- **Get thick, plush carpet.** It's comfortable and

brings the look of quality to a room—and it's not usually much more expensive.

- **Hide electrical cords to the largest possible degree.**
- **Place music devices, speakers and cords well out of sight** (mine are on top of my refrigerator).
- **Limit cabinets and bookshelves to the smallest size possible**—no large, looming shelves here or anywhere else in the home. Items on bookshelves can be arranged in matching baskets or boxes, also, to reduce the look of clutter. Better yet, experiment with keeping toys in baskets on the floor and office stuff in the office and eliminate the shelves altogether.
- **Replace clear cabinet doors with opaque ones** to reduce the look of clutter.
- **Use lightweight, plain, unpatterned curtains rather than heavy-feeling curtains or blinds**—and keep them open most of the time.
- **Make your family room a "floor-only" room, doing away with the couch.** Rediscover the bean bag; it just may change your life.
- **Get a Rumba or a non-electric carpet sweeper.** I know how much you hate to vacuum, and freshly vacuumed carpet just feels good.
- **Get matching baskets for toys and other stuff to use throughout the entire house.** These really shouldn't be see-through, and preferably not plastic, either. With so few design

elements in the Naked Home, the color and texture of these is important.

- **Try not to mix styles.** If you buy the plainest items, you won't find later that you have a Grecian-inspired shelf next to a modern couch with a 1920's-inspired painting nearby.
- **Replace floor and table lamps,** which take up floor space and feature ugly cords, with wall-mounted lamps or just good adjustable ceiling lighting, or limit your lamps to one reading lamp only per room.
- Finally, my favorite family room tip: **get rid of your coffee table.** Coffee tables are almost never empty of junk, and when they aren't they serve no purpose at all. Coffee cups can be placed on a low shelf, an upturned basket, a small tabletop with no legs, or even just a book.

The Naked Family Room is one of the most enjoyable parts of the home—but it won't be enjoyed the same way if it's full of stuff that doesn't belong.

MOLLIE PLAYER

My family room during playtime ...

THE NAKED HOUSE

*... And my family room after playtime.
Either way, it's a great place to be.*

These are the baskets I chose to use throughout my house. Because they all match (and match our hampers as well), they bring continuity to our home decor. Also, I can move them between rooms as needs change, which they very often do.

Naked Interview
Amanda Clark: "Respect the Space as a Defined Perimeter for How Much You Can Keep"

Amanda Clark is the owner or Ever So Organized ®, a full-service home organizing company based out of Orange County, California. They specialize in decluttering and creating beautiful, functional and organized systems for homeowners. See eversoorganized.com for more information.

Mollie: Have you ever significantly reorganized and decluttered your home? What led to the decision and what did you change?

Amanda: A few years ago I moved into a new home, more than doubling the square footage of the previous home. I did not declutter before the move because I was pregnant with my third baby and fairly immobile. A month into the move my third baby was born and I decluttered my entire house during my maternity leave. I no longer wanted to organize and re-organized the amount of stuff I knew I didn't even need. I wanted to enjoy the expanded space without adding more stuff in it.

Mollie: So now you actually have a large home that is spacious, too? What is that like?

Amanda: With more space in my home comes more space in my head; a weight has been lifted. I'm extremely proud of my house and it has been featured in a local publication. That never would've happened if it was filled with stuff.

Mollie: Can you share your process for decluttering?

Amanda: Look at one area at a time. For example, a pantry, closet, or even a drawer.

- Step one: Remove everything from the space. That means everything!
- Step two: Wipe down and clean the surfaces while they are empty.
- Step three: Sort like items together. You may be surprised at how many black socks, tubes of

toothpaste (you can never find) or cans of beans you own.
- Step four: Declutter. Be ruthless. Do you love it? Does it improve your life? Can you purchase it in twenty minutes for under $20 if you need it later?
- Step five: You are now allowed to shop for those pretty containers only after you know what you have left. Can risers, plastic dividers for drawers and matching slim velvet hangers really can make a big difference organizing your space. Go wild on Pinterest for ideas or check out my Instagram @eversoorganized.
- Step six: Use containers to separate items and label *everything*.
- And finally: **Respect the space as a defined perimeter for how much you can keep.** Don't cram more stuff in the space later on. Use the one-in, one-out rule to keep it under control.

Mollie: Any more tips?

Amanda: Yes!

- Turn all of your hangers backward in your closet. As you wear something replace the hanger with the cleaned item as you normally would. At the end of the season you can clearly see which clothes you have worn and which you haven't. Consider decluttering those never-worn items.
- Have a pretty bin, basket or container in a handy area. Put your mail, to-do items and even broken items you've been meaning to fix inside the container. Set aside time every single week to work

on those actionable items. If you are consistent, very few things will fall through the cracks.
- **File fold your clothes in your drawers.** This will change your life.

Mollie: What is file folding?

Amanda: File folding is a simple way of folding your clothes in a square or rectangle shape and then placing them in the drawer on their sides instead of flat. It looks similar to folders in a file cabinet. No more forgetting about what's on the bottom of your pile: now there is no bottom.

Mollie: Any final thoughts?

Amanda: Less stuff truly means more time, more money and more freedom: less time maintaining the stuff, more money in the bank account because you are buying less and more freedom from consumerism.

Naked Interview
Kelly Kandra Hughes: "Minimalism Is About Personal Growth"

Kelly Kandra Hughes has been a professional housesitter since 2016. Visit her minimalism and spirituality blog at genesispotentia.com.

Mollie: Have you ever significantly changed your life to become more minimalist? What led to the decision and what did you change?

Kelly: Yes. I got rid of approximately 95 percent of my belongings by donating, giving away, selling, recycling, or trashing them. Essentially, I wasn't happy in my current life and I wanted to make radical changes. I followed a career trajectory of which some people only dream: college, a PhD program (for which I had a full-ride scholarship), tenure track position, and tenure. Yet it wasn't the life I really wanted to live. I had all sorts of health issues related to stress and sleep. My weight dropped to 97 pounds. I developed severe adult acne. I used to hope that I would get in a nonfatal car crash, just so I could take a break from my life for a while.

It wasn't until I was granted a paid sabbatical for the 2014-2015 academic year that I finally got time to myself. I didn't miss my job for one second of one minute of one day. That was a wake-up call to me that I needed to make some changes.

While on sabbatical, and after I realized I needed to quit my job, I woke up in the middle of the night and thought, *housesitting*. I had already been pet-sitting and housesitting for friends while I was on a sabbatical. I wrote down my idea and went back to bed.

The next morning a Google search informed me that, yes, pet-sitting and housesitting is a viable way to live these days. That became my plan: to no longer have a place of my own, but to live in other people's houses. I didn't want the burden of storing of my belongings, so I made the choice to get rid of them. My husband and I have been on a long-term housesit in the northwest corner of Connecticut since September 2016. At the time we began, everything we owned fit into our car.

Mollie: What are your most prized beliefs regarding minimalist lifestyle—the ideas you want most to spread?

Kelly: The idea I most want to spread is that minimalism is not just about tidying up and reducing clutter. **It's about personal growth,** and most importantly, the understanding that there is no one way to best accomplish this growth. Being a minimalist means you have a good understanding of who you are and how you want to live your own best life ... and then acting accordingly. This understanding can be accomplished through self-reflection (e.g., journaling, creating vision boards, praying, meditating, etc.) or with the help of professionals (e.g., therapists, life coaches, pastors, career counselors, etc.).

I also want people to know that **the first thing I recommend people get rid of is mental clutter.** By knowing who you are and how you want to live your best life, you can say no to things that don't serve you. Of course, it's not easy and it takes a certain amount of courage to start saying no. But this freedom then brings benefits in other areas of your life, including increased time, energy, and financial resources to pursue the things that are most important to you.

Start by identifying your core life values. These are the five to seven values that are fundamental to who you are as person. Ask yourself questions such as, "When have I experienced the most joy in my life? When did I experience my lowest points? What happens on the days when I can't wait to get out of bed? What happens on the days where I dread getting out of bed? Who inspires me? If I could have any job in the world, what would it be and why? What did I dream of being when I was a child? If I could live a perfect day every day, what would that day look like? What are some times in my life I thought I was doing the right thing, but it turned out to be wrong for me?" Look for common themes and patterns, then name those ideas using a single word, such as *achievement, service, fairness, creativity,* or *spirituality.*

The second thing I recommend is to identify specific interests in your life related to those values. Values and interests go hand-in-hand. For example, you may value creativity, but you may have no interest in Renaissance art. If that's the case, next time you visit an art museum, give yourself the freedom to skip over entire floors and head to the impressionists who you find whimsical and inspiring. The good news is, you've probably already uncovered most of your interests if you've spent time reflecting on your core life values. Review your answers to the above questions and notice what specific activities and events are associated with your more joyful times. Keep those in mind for making your day-to-day and long-term decisions on how you're going to spend your time, effort, and money.

Mollie: I love everything you said so much. Any final thoughts, Kelly?

Kelly: Here's something that I don't think gets mentioned too often: it's important to stay open-minded and empathetic to others while living a minimalist life. I've found that people who experience the kind of personal growth that comes with minimalism are so excited about their journeys, they think their way is not only the best way, but the only way. We may end up self-righteous and judgmental of others who are still struggling on their own paths. I know I certainly did!

We need to remember where we started from and extend empathy to others who may not be there yet. When you live a life of joy and one that lines up with your core life values and interests, people become interested in what you're doing. When they ask, be happy to give advice on what worked best for you. Otherwise, it's not our place to judge. Stay focused on your own life and lead by example. I know it's cliché, but Gandhi was on to something when he said, "Be the change you wish to see in the world."

5

THE NAKED BEDROOM

THE NAKED BEDROOM IS MATCHING; or, *Oh, how I love the color brown*

I have a confession to make: I want every house in the world to be decorated entirely in brown. Okay, maybe not entirely in brown, but with brown as the base color and all other colors as accents. Brown is my favorite color and let's face it: it just makes everything look beautiful. Just ask Starbucks. They know.

If you don't feel the need to live inside a coffee shop, though, this take this piece of advice will still apply: Choose a single, soft, muted color to use throughout your entire house, then deviate not from that base come what may. If it's black, buy everything in black: towels, furniture, sheets. Choose a color that's easy to match closely across all types of products, and deviate from it only when considerable thought is given to the choice.

Here are some of the items in my home that are dark brown:

- The laundry baskets;
- All of our other storage baskets (which are in the same style as our laundry baskets);
- Our bean bags;
- Our family room carpet;
- Our living room accent wall;
- Our kitchen chair covers;
- All of our towels;
- Most of our bed sheets
- All of the top blankets on our beds (they're replicas);
- All of our curtains (again, replicas);
- All of our reusable shopping bags;
- The screensavers on my three computer monitors; and, just for fun,
- My Kindle cover, my phone background, all my favorite shirts and all of my handbags and baby carriers.

Before you rush to judgment, consider how this matching helps keep my home looking nice. Everything—the hampers, the baskets, the blankets—are completely interchangeable from room to room. Whether my husband hangs his towel to dry in the same bathroom he showers in or leaves it on the floor in the bedroom, it looks like it belongs. It blends in. It doesn't interrupt the flow of the room.

It looks less like the clutter that it is.

Single-color decor also helps inhabitants overlook small imperfections in the home: patched drywall spots suddenly don't look so patched. Nail holes in the wall suddenly don't look so holey. Paint splotches on door handles are now just minor concerns.

Even with little flaws present, the house always looks put-together.

The Naked Bedroom is bare

Sometimes, when we think back on something we did or said even just a short while ago, we find ourselves amazed that we were ever that person. When a few years back a good friend of mine casually mentioned that she and her husband had been sleeping on a mattress on the floor for over ten years, ever since their first child of four was born, my reaction is surprising to remember.

I was horrified.

"Get yourself a bed frame already!" I told her in a sort of judgmental awe.

Obviously, I knew nothing about kids, I thought when only a year later my husband and I, too, got rid of our long-used bed frame. At first, we just stored it in the garage. But not long afterwards, after Dave decided to tear out the wall the frame stood against, he consented to taking the plunge. We hauled it and our smaller full-size frame onto our front lawn and attached some signs that said "free."

They did not linger long.

And we were glad they didn't, because the arrangement worked beautifully for us. My rolling-age baby could come dangerously close to the edge of the mattress without an expletive accompaniment (though infants should never be encouraged to roll over without supervision). And later, when he started crawling and walking, the bed became his most enjoyable toy.

And it still is. These days when I think of my bedroom, I don't think of hours spent with a stack of library books, a cup of coffee and a block of empty afternoon hours, like I used to. Instead, I think of hide and seek. I think of bouncing and tickling, somersaults and airplane, and a game David likes called "baby tossing." Some of these games would be possible on a bed with a frame. But it wouldn't be possible for us to have two mattresses in the same room—one king-sized and one full—doubling the excitement and fun. It wouldn't be possible for our toddler to jump over the gap between them, or make a bridge, or to easily move from one to the other at night when half-asleep.

He might even have to have his own bedroom.

And so, Mattress Land, as we call it, works for us. But don't worry—I understand that your bedroom needs may be different. The point of this story isn't that everyone should kick their bed frames to the curb. The point is that when it comes to the bedroom, it often makes sense to think differently.

If your house is anything like ours, you don't have much square footage to spare. Why, then, reserve an entire room for a single purpose like sleeping? A guest bedroom can be a kids' room, too—or a play room, or a changing room, or a project room, or an office—or some combination of these. If you're careful about how you do it, you can have a bed, a TV, some toys and a closet full of sewing stuff and art supplies in a spare room without it feeling overly full. Three kids can play there during the day or use it to store their things, then two can sleep with Mom and Dad at night, leaving the older children with a little alone time. When the teen years hit, the bedrooms can be "owned" again, but two teens in one room is fine; they'll be alone in the world soon enough.

The flexible nature of the bedroom in mind, it would be an impossible task for me to decide what does and does not belong in yours. Instead, I'll tell you what's in view in our main bedroom, which we refer to as "the big bedroom":

- Two large mattresses;
- Matching bedding;
- Curtains;
- A dresser;
- Two matching lamps;
- Two matching lamp tables;
- Two matching hampers;
- One wall hanging; and
- Three matching baskets on the dresser.

And there you have it. Our bedroom: fun, yet functional in the extreme. Eventually, our toddler will decide to move into his own room, the "small bedroom," which he'll share with his younger brother during the day. This will double as our guest bedroom, too. After a time, the two children will share the room at night, too, one or both making frequent excursions back to our bed. If we have a third child, David and I will likely be sleeping on a mattress on the floor for well over a decade.

Here are a few additional ideas that might help you maximize your bedroom space while at the same time keeping it relatively free of clutter:

- **Use two matching hampers,** one for darks and one for lights, to reduce time spent sorting laundry.
- **Have a drawer, shelf or basket that holds only the clothes that you intend to "reuse"—to wear again before washing.** That way they don't just collect on the floor with no place in particular to go.
- **Take advantage of the potential the bedroom offers for matching.** All you need here are curtains, hampers, sheets and bedspreads of the same color to bring the room together.
- **If possible, get rid of your dresser.** Replace it with several sets of large, spacious drawers (none of those specialized small compartments, please!) to place in the bedroom closets.
- **Clean out your closet.** Regularly. (No—more often than regularly, whatever that means.) Replace the mounds of clothes you don't really love with just a few truly awesome ones you do. Personally, I find that my work wardrobe is easily managed, while my casual wardrobe is in constant flux due to its difficult-to-fulfill requirements: comfort, more comfort, and of course flattering good looks.
- **Store seasonal and temporarily unneeded clothes in the garage in moisture- and pest-proof clear boxes,** clearly labeled.
- **Don't buy fancy closet organizers.** They're impractical. Larger drawers are best—it's

easier to remember what is in there and you can always put two types of clothing in one drawer. (All my pajamas and underwear are together, for example.)

- **Try not to store anything underneath the bed.** This is just bad Feng Shui.
- **Store coats, jackets and even some sweaters, as well as your entire shoe collection, in your hallway closet, not your bedroom one.** Shoes can be placed in hanging shoe racks, not standing ones, to give the look of open floor space and to make sweeping much easier.
- **Because bedrooms are often small, not well-lit and short on windows, the Naked House rules about wall hangings (e.g., don't have them) don't always apply here.** If your bedroom needs a bit of cheering up, choose a few low-key color-coordinated hangings. Plastic frames look cheap and wooden frames with glass can sometimes feel too burdensome and heavy; therefore, I like hanging special quilts instead. You may also consider installing a special shelf for a grouping of framed pictures and knick-knacks, which often looks classier (and barer) than a wall full of pictures.
- **If you do have a large, well-lit and large-windowed bedroom, enjoy it!** Don't mess it up by hanging pictures.
- **If you absolutely can't live without a bookshelf in your bedroom, consider**

- **installing a few solid wood wall-mounted shelves to save floor space.**
- **Do consider getting rid of your bed frames, particularly if you have children.** Remember: this is your space, and your choices, no one else's.
- **There's usually no need for a bed frame with posts,** in any case, particularly if you're trying to make the room look larger.
- **Buy lamp tables with drawers or closed-door cabinets** so that you can easily keep bedside stuff (in my case, a diaper, a stack of books, a glasses cleaning cloth and the remote to the air purifier in the closet) permanently out of view.
- Kids don't necessarily need their own room for long, if at all. **Consider not buying a home with an extra bedroom if you can instead buy a smaller one** with a shorter commute. Of course, your unique family situation will determine your bedroom needs, and that's fine.

Of all of the rooms in the house, the bedroom is the place to unleash your creativity to the greatest degree—but not necessarily on paint colors or curtain styles. Instead, it's a place to use your imagination concerning the room's purpose and potential. Of course, if you don't live alone, there will very likely come a time when some of the bedroom decor decisions aren't yours to make. But that's what's so cool about the bedroom: without expensive fixtures and the like, it's the easiest room in the home to redecorate.

The bedroom is, above all, flexible—and the Naked House ideals can be, too.

The Naked Bedroom is bare. It is matching, and organized and clean, and high-quality.

And it's whatever else you want it to be.

Our bedroom, which we sometimes refer to as Mattress Land. Eventually I will repaint it and add a few high shelves, but for now I'm happy. To me, this room represents better than any other what can be achieved by merely simplifying, without purchasing anything new.

THE NAKED HOUSE

I realize that these bare walls and minimalist beds don't provide the atmosphere everybody prefers. If you choose to display more stuff in your bedroom than this, do remember that matching all the items in the room does something similar to decluttering: it eliminates visual distraction. You can always add a colorful pillow or two later if you can't stand complete uniformity. (Then change it out when that color no longer speaks to you.)

Naked Interview
Kurt Niziak: "I Lost Almost Everything in a Fire"

Kurt Niziak is a software trainer and data analyst from Massachusetts.

Mollie: Have you ever significantly reorganized and decluttered your home? What led to the decision and what did you change?

Kurt: Yes, but not consciously. Instead, it somehow chose me!

Over a decade ago, my career and financial situation was vastly different. In fact, my own "personal paper route" (as I call it) was surprisingly easy. Financially, I was preparing myself for a life of moderate wealth. The bottom fell out, however, and I was forced to abide by a lifestyle which would be the antitheses of what I once thought I had.

In July of 2018, I had a major fire in my once well-furnished condo. I had stepped out of my home for a mere thirty-five minutes only to return and witness that almost all of what I had acquired over the years had vanished. I say the word *almost* because, my most important possession (my dog) was miraculously spared. (Thank God).

After the complete shock of losing almost everything had slowly worn off, I was surprised to feel an incredible sense of gratitude. I realized that as terrible as things were, at least my dog was okay. This horrific event proved to be the genesis of a priceless awakening. I began to understand that I really didn't need many possessions in order to keep on living on a day-to-day basis. Material things somehow revealed themselves in their most generic form, serving as nothing more than distractions.

Mollie: What is your lifestyle like now?

Kurt: I suppose that I am a bit more grounded. I am cognizant about how we are all such insatiable consumers. I try instead to take better care of the things that I do have, rather than fantasizing about what I don't have. Furthermore, before purchasing or storing anything, I think about whether I really need it.

We all are conditioned to believe that our lives can only improve via addition—as if we were painting a picture, adding more and more layers. Unfortunately, this approach seldom gets us the results we are looking for. Perhaps it's a sculpture that we should be creating instead, our goal only arrived at via subtraction. We discard the pieces that are not necessary.

Mollie: Can you share a few specific tips for cleaning, organizing and simplifying a home?

Kurt: In his wonderful book *12 Rules of Life: An Antidote to Chaos,* Jordan Peterson is quick to point out an approach towards minimalism which (at first look) appears rather benign. However, this simple concept has saved me, time and time again, from the shackles of a personal two- or three-day funk. Peterson states that one risks feeling depressed, anxious and powerless should they fail to keep their bedroom clean, or surroundings in order. Whenever I motivate myself to use this simple tactic, it has never failed to make me feel more balanced—more in control.

Cleaning, organizing, etc. are extremely powerful minimalist tools. They help combat feelings of chaos. If things are clean and in order, I have a better chance at having a more positive experience in the outside world. Physical clutter seems to muddle my brain and often prevents me from having any semblance of harmony. It is so simple, yet it seems to always have positive results.

Minimalism (to me) is not merely the act of owning less. It also leads to appreciating things more. It proves itself, time and time again, as a powerful life approach. All I know is that when I fail to encompass minimalism, I am at risk of feeling like nothing more than the proverbial hole of a doughnut.

I will say however, that my own personal happiness has neither significantly decreased nor increased over the years. It is just less complicated. One doesn't end up wasting time fooling themselves into thinking that acquiring more will improve one's life.

I do what I need to do in order to survive. I often (jokingly) say that I am just as miserable now, as I've always been. A bigger house, better car or more stuff will not enhance my life very much. These things might be nice to have but it becomes a fool's errand to obsessively pursue. It's just an example of victory through surrender.

6

THE NAKED BATHROOM

EVEN IN THE NAKED HOUSE, buying new stuff can be awesome

I still remember the day I discovered that new, unstained kitchen rags came in ten-packs that cost a dollar.

It happened when I was in college. I was shopping at the local dollar store, and I wasn't looking for rags—and yet, when I saw them sitting there on the shelf next to the Ajax, I stopped dead in my tracks. *I can't believe what my eyes they are a-seeing*, I thought. *Ten perfectly absorbent, high-quality bright white rags, cheaper to obtain than a large soda.*

I quickly grabbed five packs.

I enjoyed the rags, thinking always of my good bargain when I used them. However, the real value of the purchase was the lesson it taught—even though it didn't sink in till later.

When I married my first husband, my bleach-stained, mismatched towels—including the one I bought while living in China that I carted home with me halfway across the globe—married, too. Their partners were my new husband's family's hand-me-downs (two sets of two: one blue-and-white striped, one plain green). One day, though, bored and roaming the nearby Kmart as unemployed housewives sometimes do, I found them: good quality plain white towels of the Martha Stewart lineage—cheap, and cheaper still since on sale.

I bought four. I brought them home and did the unthinkable, the act that in all my life my mother had never even once considered: I threw out the worst of our old towels. I didn't cut them up into rags, like my mom would've done—I just tossed them into the garbage.

When I separated from my husband, those four white towels traveled halfway across the country in my suitcase, joining me on my next adventure. (Apparently, towels are my security blankets. It's Freudian.) Then, when recently I completed my new home's all-brown towel collection with some lovely $10 additions, I gave those white towels to my mother.

She cut them up into rags.

The moral of these stories: stuff really isn't that expensive. When I consider how many years I chose to make do with worn-out, ugly objects in my daily environment and visual space—well, I'm just a little bit shocked. Some of these items may have been too expensive for me to replace at the time, but others I kept for one reason, and one reason alone, namely: I was used to them.

Which is why, even though I so strongly advocate minimalism, I'm not going to tell you to never buy new things. Whereas some people think that it's unwise to shop too much, to bring new stuff into your life, I say that the problem is not buying new stuff; the problem is refusing to then throw the old stuff away.

Consider this: if you allow yourself to buy nice new things on occasion, it may be easier for you to let go of the junk.

And the word "junk" here is no exaggeration. No matter how nice you think that old computer case is, if it won't sell on Craigslist it's probably not worth your keeping it, either.

In the sociology classic *The Paradox of Choice,* author Barry Schwartz makes an insightful point. He says that generally speaking, people greatly overvalue the stuff they already own, and fairly value stuff they do not. He calls it *loss aversion,* and it's the reason most people feel worse about unexpectedly losing $100 than they feel good about unexpectedly gaining the same amount.

In other words: if tomorrow you came across that beautiful red pillow that no longer matches your decor in a garage sale giveaway pile rather than in your own linen closet, you wouldn't think twice about passing it up.

Certainly this is true of clothes. No matter how many wearables I give away each year (and believe me, it is more than a few), in the left-hand corner of the top shelf of my clothes closet a little collection of stuff I just can't seem to let go of remains, despite the contents' itchiness or too-small size.

The Naked Bathroom is bare and matching

However, as this is the bathroom chapter, not the bedroom one, let us explore the skeletons not in our closets, but instead those under our sinks.

Here are a few of the most common necessary (in some cases arguably necessary) bathroom toiletries that steal the square footage of the smallest room in the house:

- Toilet paper;
- Towels currently in use;
- Backup towels;
- Toothpaste, toothbrushes and other mouth care items currently in use;
- Backup toothpaste, toothbrushes and other mouth care items;
- Diapers;
- Feminine hygiene products;
- Soap currently in use;
- Backup soap;
- Lotion currently in use;
- Backup lotion;
- Shampoo, conditioner and other hair products currently in use;
- Backup shampoo, conditioner and other hair products;
- Hair dryers, curlers and the like;
- Makeup currently in daily use;
- Extra makeup for special occasions;
- Jewelry;
- Combs and various hair decorations;
- A scale;
- A trash can;
- Bathroom cleaning supplies and air freshener;

- A plunger; and
- Vitamins and medicine.

All of these items are important. All of these items have their proper place in the Naked House.

But only about half of them belong in the bathroom.

Can you guess which half is which? The answer is simple: any of these items that are not used daily can be stored elsewhere. In addition, bathroom cleaning supplies can be stored with the rest of the home's cleaning supplies, in order to lessen the number of bottles and implements needed (and to keep them secured away from children). And in my home, vitamins and medicines have their own cabinet in the kitchen, where use of them is much more convenient. Jewelry may be kept in the bedroom and the plunger can be kept in the garage. Backup towels can be kept in the linen closet, and all of the other backup items can be kept in neatly labeled, clean, clear storage boxes in an accessible location in the garage.

That's right: alongside my admonition to please buy matching towels and new rags, for goodness' sake, my favorite tip for simplifying the bathroom is this: take all the junk out from under your sink and put it in the garage.

Need a bit more inspiration? Following are all of the items—each and every last one—that sit on the counter in my guest bath:

- A small basket of clean single-use hand towels;
- A small matching basket of used single-use hand towels; and
- A bar of soap.

Here are all of the items that currently sit on the counter in my master bath, and that after our upcoming bathroom remodel will almost without exception be stored in a small cabinet over the sink instead:

- Toothbrushes in a glass;
- My electric toothbrush and its stand;
- My husband's electric water pick;
- Soap;
- A basket containing my husband's razors, some lotion, floss, a lens cleaning cloth and some Q-tips; and
- A basket containing my husband's contacts and contact solution and our deodorant.

Similarly, here are all of the items in my guest bath cabinets under the sink:

- Diapers;
- Toilet paper;
- A baby scale; and
- Bath toys.

And here are all of the items in my master bath cabinets:

- Toilet paper (yes, really only that)

Everything else—my sewing kits, my old hair products, even the few pieces of (cheap) jewelry I own—are stored in a single clear plastic box in the garage that's marked "toiletries."

And this one change has made all the difference.

Now, I should tell you that other than keeping your bathroom relatively clean and such, most of my bathroom-maximizing tips are a bit less gratifying—and quite a bit more expensive—than these two. So take it or leave it as you like when I say that when Dave and I remodel our bathrooms, here are the changes we (okay, I) plan to make:

- **We will get a deeper-than-normal (but not necessarily wider than normal) bathtub.** The ideal bathtub easily covers two or three people with water. When only one person is in it, less water can be used (unlike with wider Jacuzzi-type tubs).
- **We would love to install full-room drainage.** Theoretically, this would mean the kids are free to splash in the bathtub to their hearts' content—an ease-of-living improvement that will be appreciated for years to come.
- **We'd add a high-end, super quiet fan.** (How often does a noisy fan interrupt your bath time reverie?)
- **We'd install a stand-alone sink (or two) with no cabinets underneath.** This serves two purposes: first, to give the illusion of greater floor space, helping to provide that "spa feel" we're after; and second, to eliminate the possibility of counter top clutter.
- **We'd have a limited number of cabinets placed at eye-level or above,** again to increase floor space. (One is a good number.)
- **We'd add a single small cabinet over the sink** that holds all of the frequently-needed stuff.

- **We'd keep a good deal of space between the toilet and the bathtub,** so that it is not within easy view during your relaxing soak.
- **We'd get that square toilet** I was telling you about. For sure.

The perfect bathroom is a difficult thing to find. Ideally, the bathroom is as relaxing, functional and beautiful as every other room in your home, providing a spacious, clean and spa-like atmosphere.

Fortunately, since most of your time is spent elsewhere, a perfect bathroom need not be your priority; rather, keep the one you have clean and tidy. Take it from atmosphere-conscious me when I say that having an ugly bathroom really isn't all that bad, but peeing in a dirty toilet is.

THE NAKED HOUSE

This is a fixture that I hate. It offers poor, glaring light, but what I'm really offended by during bath time is its looks. Though not of the most over-the-top variety, its few ornate, mock-fancy design elements are much more distracting to the eye than one might realize at first. And because the style doesn't match the rest of the home's hardware, or the design aesthetic in general, it's glaringly (!) obvious why someone chose it: it was cheap.

> Since we haven't updated our bathrooms yet, I'm left with a back splash that looks like a last-minute decision. Picturing this old counter top without the harsh, angular tile reminds me of how much aesthetic damage can be done by a single unnecessary, messy addition.

Naked Interview

Haley Gallerani: "I Brought Two Suitcases with Me and Two Suitcases Back"

Haley Gallerani runs The Vegan Abroad, a website about traveling sustainably and as a vegan. Visit it at theveganabroadblog.com.

Mollie: Have you ever significantly minimized your possessions? What led to the decision and what did you change?

Haley: I would say that I officially became a minimalist in 2018 when I moved to Chiang Mai, Thailand. I brought two suitcases with me and two suitcases back. I knew that I wouldn't be living in Thailand forever so I didn't want to purchase too many things while I was there. I did have to purchase a few things for my apartment, but it came furnished so my purchases were minimal.

The biggest way that I minimized my possessions was with my clothing. I used to own so many clothing pieces that I hardly ever wore. I now rotate among around ten different outfits. My biggest tip for simplifying your wardrobe is to **only purchase neutral colors**. This will allow you to mix and match more than if you own clothing with different colors and patterns.

Mollie: What is your life like now? How often do you travel and for how long? Do you still take only two suitcases?

Haley: I have been in the United States for the past few months, but I will be moving to Europe in January 2020. I am a big believer in slow travel. That means that I spend a long time in one location before moving onto the next. Europe is a bit more complicated than Thailand because of visa issues. I will start in Italy where I will stay for three months: one month in Rome, one month in Florence, and one month in Sicily. Then I will be going to Croatia for three months before finally settling in the Czech Republic where I will get a visa.

I am planning on only bringing one suitcase and a backpack with me to Europe because I will be moving around so much. I know that this is going to be even more challenging since Europe has four different seasons that I need to pack clothes for whereas it was almost always summer temperatures in Thailand. I am excited about the challenge, though, and I think that I will grow even more minimalist.

Mollie: What are your most prized beliefs regarding minimalist lifestyle—the ideas you most want to spread?

Haley: My most prized belief regarding a minimalist lifestyle is that there isn't a one-size-fits-all for minimalism. I think that you have to find what brings you joy in life and focus on that. Clothing doesn't bring me joy, so that is a very easy area for me to be a minimalist in. I do love cooking, though, so someone could look at my kitchen and think that I am not a minimalist, but then look at my closet and think that I am. Ultimately, I think that minimalism is about focusing on the things that matter to you, and spending less time (and money) on the things that don't. When you find the things that don't bring you joy, get rid of them.

Also, try to find ways to simplify the things that do bring you joy. For example, I am an avid reader. I only purchased physical books prior to moving to Thailand. I decided to purchase a Kindle before moving to Thailand so I could easily purchase books in English while I was abroad. It ended up being one of the best purchases that I have ever made because I no longer have the clutter of books anymore, and I can fit hundreds of books on a very small device.

Mollie: Any final thoughts?

Haley: Becoming a minimalist can be scary at first as you are getting rid of a bunch of your possessions. The thought of "What if I need this in the future?" may show up. **My advice would be to keep the item that you are questioning for six months to a year depending on what the item is.** If you haven't used it in that time then you should probably get rid of it.

7

THE NAKED GARAGE

GARAGES ARE INSPIRING, I swear

Last spring, I experienced something amazing—and pretty ordinary as well: I cleaned out my garage.

It was a project that took all spring to complete.

One afternoon in the midst of this, I was watching my young child become engrossed in a box of tools in a way he'd never been with his regular toys when suddenly, it hit me: *We're having a really good time. He's in his zone: screwing with screwdrivers and hammering with hammers and examining every facet of the motorcycle.*

But I'm actually having fun, too.

And it's true; I was. I was pleasantly challenged by the task of ensuring each item in the garage found a dedicated, clearly labeled home. I was enjoying the re-labeling, the re-stacking, the re-sorting, the re-categorizing. I got to relive a bit of my past while making sure it would be protected for the future. After a time, the whole endeavor took on a life of its own, starting with a bit of straightening up and morphing into a monumental effort that by season's end enabled us to park our car in the garage for the first time since owning our house.

And so, for a while after that, I got a little excited about garages. Soon after the task was complete, I took up a terrible new habit (okay, maybe not entirely new, but definitely terrible): I started embarrassing myself at dinner parties.

See, approximately one Saturday evening each month my husband and I host a dinner or game night at our house. We love the quality time we get to spend with our friends in this way—and they love not having to cook. But starting around the time of the Epic Garage Makeover, it happened: I started cajoling our guests into taking unexpected excursions to our garage—garage tours, so to speak.

Now, admittedly, the roots of the problem had taken hold before this time. I had long enjoyed expressing my ideas on the importance of good flooring, my hatred of tile and my theory that all bathrooms should have full room drainage—no matter what the company or occasion. And when the subject leaned even remotely toward home organization, it was even worse. I have opened my kitchen cabinets to illustrate a point about Pyrex (see "The Naked Kitchen"). I have had inappropriately long discussions in my bedroom with other peoples' husbands about our home's lack of bed frames. And the advantages of bean bags are not unknown to most of our family and friends.

But when I actually started dragging our guests into the garage to show them what I'd recently accomplished there, I realized that a line had been crossed. (I'm working on it, okay?)

Here's the thing, though: I'm not the only one to be fascinated with this interesting, uniquely purposeful home location.

Consider this example: the other month, a friend of mine held "space camp" in her garage. After decking out the place with the rarest of rarities and the nicest of niceties—including walk-in-sized cardboard boxes, old motorcycle helmets and mismatched gloves—she invited a group of kids aged three to seven over to play.

And they stayed all afternoon. See, there's something little people (and many moms) understand that the rest of us seem to miss: the garage is a wonderful place to be. It's a place of motorcycles and cars. It's a place of tools and tool chests, toys and toy chests that resemble treasure chests in many key ways. It's a place of sports equipment of all kinds and varieties, of boxes filled with almost anything you can imagine.

You can get dirty in the garage. You can use the garden hose if you need to, and get wet. You can do impossible things there, like building and collecting and investigating ... and most anything else. The possibilities are endless, and the ideas flow easily and fast.

In short: the garage is one very inspiring place.

And it's not just children that feel it—we adults are nearly as susceptible to its charms, though often in an unconscious way. Some of us use it to build and create, others to sing in a band. Some of us think of garage organization as a serious hobby, while others just appreciate this location's unique ability to keep some of our most relied-upon possessions safe.

Whatever your perspective may be on your garage, I hope this chapter encourages you to take better advantage of this special space, to help it fulfill its potential.

And maybe the most significant aspect of that potential is this: it can enable you to have a Naked House.

The Naked Garage isn't bare—but it is the apex of organized

As I argued already, things don't cost what they cost; they cost what they cost to buy, maintain, move around and store. And there's no better place to demonstrate that truth than in the prized real estate of your garage.

For this reason, the basic Naked Garage organization philosophy is as follows: the garage is not a place to store all the junk you can't bear to throw out. Instead, with its plentiful space, few aesthetic concerns and ease of access, the garage is a vital part of the Naked House. It serves as not just the main, but the only real storage area—even for things you use on a regular basis. This way, the rest of the home may be pruned back to only the necessities.

Now, realistically speaking, your garage will never be perfect; stuff will sit in there for years that you think you'll need but never do. After all, who can talk a stubborn husband into getting rid of all his lame DVDs? (You can try, of course, but please be gentle and take it slow. A Naked Garage isn't worth a heated argument, just a cheerful nag here and there.)

Nevertheless, it's almost certainly possible to get rid of a whole bunch of stuff in your garage, and to beautifully organize all the rest.

Here are my tips for doing just that:

- **Create a "box wall,"** a single garage wall that is easily accessible and can accommodate small- to medium-sized everyday items. If possible, put the boxes on shelves; if not, just stack 'em on up.
- **Label boxes clearly.** I know, I know, it's a pain. But the effort will pay off, I promise.
- **Under-fill boxes.** This is one of the more difficult garage ideals to achieve. However, when later you need to add items of the same type to the box, or just find something you put in it, you'll be glad you didn't cram.
- **Get a ton of boxes.** I keep going back to the store to buy more.
- **Use clear boxes.**
- **Buy boxes that are moisture- and rodent-proof**—not the cheapest boxes you can find, particularly for stuff that's susceptible to damage. Cardboard boxes aren't good enough for the things that you enjoy enough to keep. (Besides, they probably won't be of uniform size.)
- **Consider leaving one box empty.** The empty box is something like the empty space in a sliding puzzle: it gives you flexibility, room to maneuver and reshape the wall.
- **Buy boxes in just one or two sizes,** which will make stacking easier, and will provide flexibility when reorganizing later on. Also, a wall

THE NAKED HOUSE

of same-size boxes looks more organized, which subconsciously encourages people to keep it that way.

- **Make the switch to ebooks.** Or do what I do: borrow the hard copy from the library, then buy the ebook later on if you want to make it a permanent part of your collection. Hard copies you've already read can be passed on to others, of course. And as with all the other guidelines in this book, exceptions may be made here; reference books may be worth their heft, and we have lots of kids' books in our family room.
- **Scan and digitize all of your photos.** This process saved me at least two storage boxes worth of space—and our pictures are now better-preserved, better-organized and much more accessible.
- If you have kids, **repurpose some of the stuff in the garage into toys.** Kids love real, adult stuff like nothing else.
- **Keep an in/out box near the garage door** for items that you plan to return to their dedicated boxes when time permits. It's a weird little idiosyncrasy of mine that I'm ridiculously proud of the in/out box in my garage. (Humility is not my strong suit, okay?)
- **Organize the garage frequently.** Don't get too attached to your first stab at logically combining all your stuff into those beautiful new boxes. Reorganize as often as your collections grow and shrink.
- **Purge the garage even more frequently.**

The things I wish I hadn't thrown out could probably be counted on five fingers. (A favorite jacket with a broken zipper that I should've just had fixed, and the key for a ski rack we never use but could have sold are the only two that come to mind.)

- **Don't spend a lot of time getting the box labels just right.** Slap up some tape and write on it. If you're doing the Naked Garage right, the box labels will change regularly.
- **Label your garage shelving in a grid format: A-Z one direction and 1-10 another.** That way, when your spouse asks where his motorcycle gloves are again, you don't have to give a full description such as, "They're in the black medium-sized box on the large box wall about one in from the garage door and about two shelves from the top." Instead, you can say, "2B."

In order to better illustrate the Naked Garage, I offer you this virtual tour (sans crackly megaphone) of the boxes in my own garage, with each phrase representing one box.

Medium-sized clear totes:

- **Bottom-level (least accessible) boxes:** Books; books; CDs and DVDs; books.
- **Level two boxes:** Books, books, CDs and DVDs; my husband's personal memorabilia.
- **Level three boxes:** Photos, my personal

memorabilia; computer stuff and electronics; holiday and craft items.
- **Top-level (most accessible) boxes:** Chemicals; giveaways and other people's stuff; toiletries; an empty box.

The most useful boxes of these: toiletries, other people's stuff (how long do you want that borrowed book to sit on your desk awaiting the next visit?), and computer stuff.

Oversized opaque totes:

- **Bottom-level boxes:** Empty product boxes; empty product boxes; my husband's miscellaneous stuff.
- **Level two boxes:** Camping stuff, snowboarding stuff, miscellaneous stuff.
- **Top-level boxes:** Skating and biking stuff, cords, miscellaneous sports stuff.

The most useful box here: the cords. We are always, it seems, changing out or adding electric cords.

Our second box wall, recently added, includes a box of painting supplies, tools too large for our large rolling tool chest; electrical supplies; car supplies (including gas cans and snow chains); work clothing; and kids' clothing we may one day use again. We also store large items (our lawn mower, saws, work tables, snowboards, bicycles and more) in the garage, though I'd like to get one of those cute pre-fab sheds for this stuff someday.

Think of your garage as a continuous work in progress. As your stuff comes, goes, shrinks and grows, your storage boxes will get reused, reassigned and reorganized. The garage isn't meant to be a stale, moldy, scary place where your stuff goes to either die or get lost. Instead, it is a living, breathing space—one that is appreciated as much as any other room in the home. People who have a Naked House visit their garages every day, retrieving and replacing sewing kits, carpet cleaner, library books and other borrowed items that are on the way back to their source.

Embrace your garage. Visit it and interact with it often and with delight.

Allow it to be the place of inspiration it wants to be.

THE NAKED HOUSE

I think the beauty of my box wall speaks for itself, really.

**Naked Interview
Kelly Rupiper: "Take a Hard Look at Your Calendar"**

Kelly Rupiper is Content Director at Upparent, a recommendation-sharing website for parents. She is also the mother of two elementary school-aged kids. See Upparent.com.

Mollie: Have you ever significantly reorganized and decluttered your home? What led to the decision and what did you change?

Kelly: Parenthood brings with it a lot of stuff. When my kids were a newborn and a toddler, we moved from a small condo into a larger home and it felt like the floodgates for accumulating toys, clothes, and gear were opened. It was easy to add more and more stuff now that we had the room, and though I don't think we had gone overboard by common standards, eventually I started feeling like we were spending too much time putting away toys, sorting through piles of clothes, and generally cleaning up. **The effort that we were putting into taking care of all of these things was more than the happiness we were getting out of having them.** This was around the time that people started talking more about a minimalist lifestyle, and the idea of letting go of the clutter seemed freeing to me. I spent the better part of a year combing through our home and putting together donations, selling items on Facebook, and handing things down to family members. A few years later we embarked on a cross-country move, and this was a great opportunity to think critically about what really needed to come with us and pare down some more.

Mollie: What are your most prized beliefs regarding minimalist lifestyle—the ideas you most want to spread?

Kelly: A minimalist lifestyle isn't just about owning as little as possible or going without. It's about limiting yourself to the things that are important, special, and useful to you, and getting to enjoy these things every day because you're not weighed down by needing to weed through and maintain all of the fluff.

It's also not just about physical belongings. **Think about taking a more minimal approach to the way you schedule your family's time and attention, too.** Take a hard look at all of the after-school activities and obligations on your calendar, and think about how it would feel to spend less time driving around and more time at home as a family.

Mollie: Tell me more about the benefits of minimizing one's schedule.

Kelly: Aside from keeping more money in the bank and enjoying more family time together, I have found that minimizing the number of activities that kids have on their plates helps to keep them from getting burned out. My kids tend to get overwhelmed when the schedule gets to the point where we're running from one activity to the next, and lessening their load means they can actually look forward to the things they've signed up for.

Mollie: Why do you think people have a hard time being at home with no planned activity?

Kelly: There's an instinct to feel like we have to entertain our kids, and the choruses of "I'm bored!" don't help. But when kids aren't overwhelmed by a playroom stuffed with endless choices and instead have a small collection of toys that inspire open-ended play, it's pretty amazing to see how well they can entertain themselves and each other without parental intervention.

Mollie: How can people learn to embrace unplanned family time?

Kelly: **Simple, low-key family traditions can be a great way to give some structure to your family time without introducing outside obligations.** My family does a weekly Friday night family movie night and we rotate the person who gets to pick what we watch. The kids look forward to it all week. We are also reading the Harry Potter series together, and we sit down to read a chapter most evenings after the kids are showered and ready for bed. Introducing fun (and often free!) activities like these gives the family something easy to do together that they look forward to and creates memories that you'll be able to enjoy for years.

Mollie: Can you share a few specific tips for simplifying a home?

Kelly: Do what you can to keep excess things from coming into your house in the first place. Getting your family on board with this will make it much easier. It's hard to deny well-meaning relatives who love to buy gifts for your kids, so give them ideas that mesh well with minimalism: a museum membership, a kids cooking class, or one larger-ticket holiday gift (like a basketball hoop or a streaming service membership) for the whole family to enjoy together. My kids will often choose a special family experience like an amusement park trip or theater tickets instead of a large birthday party with friends and gifts.

Mollie: Any final thoughts?

Kelly: Minimalism isn't just about clearing out your house. It's about changing your mindset, so you're better-equipped to maintain your new way of life moving forward. Once you discover and embrace how freeing it is to be living without the clutter in your house and on your calendar, it's easier to be able to say "no" to the pressure we all feel to take on more.

8

MORE NAKED

MY HOUSE ISN'T REALLY ALL that nice; it's just empty

I get a good number of compliments on my house. Which might seem a bit strange when you consider that, relatively speaking, it isn't really all that nice. It's one of many average-looking homes on an average-looking street in a pretty average-looking neighborhood (much improved by the numerous coniferous trees, which I dearly love). Most of the houses were, like mine, built in the 1950s or '60s. None of them except the remodels are large, and many, like my 1500-square footer, are of rather modest size. One of my neighbors hasn't cleaned his roof in thirty-nine years or so; it's all but invisible under a thick layer of clumpy moss. Another has changed nothing about his home's appearance in much longer, including the exact position of the 1976 Ford pickup parked under the carport, trusting nature's grand but gentle touch to make all needed aesthetic improvements. And one of my former neighbors used to hoard relatives (and their cars) like gallon jugs of water in a drought.

Which is why I love it.

There's something special about non-specialness, isn't there? My home, and my neighborhood, are modest. There's some personality, some character here, even though it's firmly suburban. (Also, my neighbors don't mind when I leave my garbage out on the curb a few extra days. This I appreciate.)

My home, like the neighborhood in which it resides, is ordinary indeed. So what do my friends mean when they say that it's nice? I think they mean that it seems well-organized and well-cared for, and that it has a calm, peaceful feel. It's also fairly clean most of the time. But most of all, it's empty.

It seems likely that it's this emptiness that most inspires admiration.

The solution is almost always fewer things. That's the Naked House philosophy in a nutshell, and there's a good reason for that: freedom from clutter is the foundation of the four principles that follow. When a room is bare, it's easy to organize, and even easier to clean. When it's bare, matching the items you do have isn't difficult. And when it's bare, the few high-quality items you really need are together more affordable than would be everything else.

This goal in mind, I offer a few Naked House tips regarding rooms I haven't elsewhere discussed. Following this, I share several non-room-specific ideas—important simple living strategies that apply to multiple locations in the home, or to one's life more generally.

. . .

Tips for getting even more naked

- **The Naked Dining Room:** Dining rooms are for dining tables—period. No shelves, no display cabinets and absolutely no paperwork, books and the like. If you don't have an office and like to use the dining table for work, set aside a clearly separated corner somewhere else in the home for a desk and your basic office supplies. Keep all of the papers and supplies in the desk's drawers (no pencil containers or paper trays, please), and store any overflow in the garage.
- **The Naked Hallway:** Again, less is more. Hallways and entryways should be entirely free of furniture, wall hangings and, well, anything else. I love the feeling I have when in the morning I open my bedroom door for the first time that day ... and see nothing but a long, empty hallway leading to a clean, open living room.
- **The Naked Closet:** Try not to overcrowd your precious closet space. Use it only for often-used items, particularly the aforementioned coats and shoes, and store most everything else in the garage. (There are a few exceptions, such as anything that is susceptible to mice and too large for waterproof containers, like suitcases). Floors are best kept bare, with shoes kept on hanging shoe organizers, not clunky floor racks.
- **The Naked Yard:** The Naked Yard philosophy is different from the Naked Home philosophy in that here, it's best to let nature rule. Rather than pruning back your trees and

bushes and keeping a perfectly manicured lawn, consider simplifying your yard upkeep by planting moss or clover rather than grass, hardy flowers like tulips and crocuses in beds, not flower pots, and letting a little wildness in. Curves are good and so are hills, and keep as much green as possible. Remove as many harsh lines and demarcations (like wooden plant bed markers) as possible so that one section of the lawn flows naturally into the other. Here, if you like, fill the empty spaces with more plants rather than keeping a wide-open lawn. If you have kids, don't worry about keeping the yard free of toys—this is a place to let them use their imaginations. Also, eat outside as a family whenever possible. Personally, when it comes to time and money spent on home improvements and chores, I prioritize the inside of the home over the outside, feeling that our trees and moss-crowded lawn make our yard a beautiful, peaceful place all on their own.

- **The Naked Den, Workroom or Office.** If you're like me, you like having one room in the house that doesn't require perfect neatness every day—a place to store that odd item that is making a temporary appearance in the home and doesn't belong anywhere else. If that is the case, I say make that room the office. Use it as a place to have that bookshelf you eschewed elsewhere, filled to the brim with relevant, important stuff (and maybe a favorite knick-knack or two as well).

- **The Naked Pantry.** The pantry is the perfect place to keep your utilities as well as your extra food. If you don't have a pantry, you'll probably want a set of utility drawers somewhere anyway. Trust me when I say that when your partner asks where the batteries are, you'll be glad you took the time.

General tips

Finally, here are a few tips from the field that, though important, are not room-specific.

- If you tend to forget to pay bills or answer mail on time, **keep all of your mail in a single box and sort it regularly.**
- If you have kids or even regular kid visitors, **childproof your drawers, cabinets, outlets and, well, everything else.** Your time with the little ones will be so much more fun and relaxed.
- **Consider employing three of the most common household tips from Feng Shui experts:** incorporate a sense of nature, reduce hard edges, protect the back (make sure sitting places don't expose people's backs to others), and use good lighting.
- **Keep your curtains open most of the time.** While you're at it, open your windows, too.
- **Kits—boxes of items that you normally use together such as hair care supplies—can come in handy.**

- **Remove tags from everything: appliances, furniture, curtains, whatever.** The room will be just that much less messy looking.
- **Consider purchasing a large set of matching oversize sandals and distributing them at each door of the house.** This makes quick trips outside easier and encourages people not to wear shoes inside.

Your home can be a better, barer place. It may even help you find peace

It's a strange fact but a fact nonetheless: most people greatly underestimate the effect of their environment on their mood and enjoyment of life.

I don't know why this is. Shouldn't we have figured it out by now? We pay three times the normal price of wine, just so we can drink it on an uncomfortable stool in a sexy, cool bar. We do the same with coffee at Starbucks. And we spend a whole load of cash to sit by a pool in Mexico, rather than the one at the local YMCA.

We think we have other reasons for doing these things, reasons that are much more logical and detached. The bar is convenient. Starbucks has free Wi-Fi. And in Mexico you can scuba dive or ride a horse.

But home is convenient. Home has the internet, and there are bodies of water and horses here, too. We don't go for any of that; we go because we want to get away.

Our homes can't give us that getaway experience, of course, but they can offer something even better: an ongoing sense of well-being in our everyday life.

Allow me to say again what I said in chapter one: Your home is like a person—and, like a person, it has a soul.

It can speak to you. It can communicate with you. It can make you feel something unique.

Of course, I don't blame you for not behaving like my aforementioned spiritual gurus and speaking back—or for thinking I'm a bit kooky for even mentioning the idea. But I do hope that reading this book has helped you think about your home's potential in a different way. I hope you've seen that the atmosphere in which you spend the majority of your time can make a difference in your life. It can comfort you. It can calm you.

It can even help you find peace.

THE NAKED HOUSE

My dining room: if it weren't for the antique bar by the wall, it would be perfectly naked. (Alas, spouses' feelings for their grandmothers must be considered at times.)

MOLLIE PLAYER

One of the small pleasures of having a Naked Home is opening my bedroom door to this clean, fresh-feeling hallway every morning.

Naked Interview
Mary Cornetta

Mary Cornetta co-owns Sort and Sweet, Inc., a luxury home organizing company which services Long Island, NY, Malibu, CA and Atlanta, GA. You can find her at SortandSweetNY.com.

Mollie: Have you ever significantly reorganized and decluttered your home? What led to the decision and what did you change?

Mary: I grew up in a home that was pretty cluttered and whether it was because of that environment or just the way that I am as a person, I decided I didn't want that lifestyle for myself once I moved out on my own. There was a period of time in my twenties that I became extremely minimalist to the point that it was almost detriment (not having enough clothing options to choose from to go to work, for example!). I would actually stress myself out over things and couldn't relax knowing that there was one spoon in the sink to be cleaned.

Now, in my thirties, as someone who owns a professional organizing company, I've learned that there is a happy medium. I'm more lenient on myself when it comes to clutter, especially during busy times with the business, and if something spark joy plus I use it on a regular basis/have the space for it, I keep it! I do not hold onto things that don't serve a purposes (even if I *might* need it one day, there's always Amazon at my fingertips) nor things that I don't really love.

Mollie: Can you give me an example?

Mary: A quick example is that I really love shoes but am not crazy about bags. I own maybe two handbags and the rest of the space that bags would've taken up, is where I store my dozens of shoes that I swap out and wear regularly. I've found that if you really love and will use something, make the space for it but if you don't, there's no reason to have it in your home.

Being minimalist should not make you feel deprived and clutter shouldn't stress you out. Finding that harmonious balance is where I strive to be in my home and my life at all times.

Mollie: What are your most prized beliefs regarding minimalist lifestyle—the ideas you want most to spread?

Mary: Much like what I spoke of above, I try to instill in my clients a sense of having a home and life you love and that it should represent quality over quantity. Holding onto things because you think you might need them again one day or because you feel guilty of letting go or because all of your neighbors have it, isn't a way to live or set an example for your children. Being a minimalist means that you own all that you need and want and nothing more.

Mollie: Can you share a few very specific tips for cleaning, organizing and simplifying a home or for living a successful minimalist lifestyle?

Mary: A few tips that I like to give for simplifying a home and successfully living a minimalist lifestyle are as follows:

- Always ask yourself three questions before you buy anything: first, "Do I love it?" Second, "Will I use/wear it often?" Third, "Do I have space to store it?" If you cannot confidently answer yes to

all three of those questions, resist the urge to buy the thing!
- Have tidying routines that you stick to every day, such as making your bed as soon as you get out of it, opening and sorting the mail at least a few times per week, not going to sleep without cleaning up the kitchen, etc. By making it a habit, you will do it automatically and your home will be tidier and your life easier than someone who lets stuff pile up.
- Follow the one-in, one-out rule which means that for every new item you bring into your house, one has to go. For example, if you buy a new pair of jeans, one pair you currently own has to go out for donation. This prevents you from having too much of one type of item and cuts down on the stress of clutter.

Naked Interview
Ben Soreff: "Nothing Good Comes Out of Chaos"

Ben Soreff is a professional home organizer at House to Home Organizing. Read more about his company at h2horganizing.com.

Mollie: What was the most cluttered home you worked in like? How did the process of organizing affect your client?

Ben: We have seen everything from estates to apartments, but the only clutter difference is the volume. In some cases, no room is being used for its intended purpose: the cars can't go in the garage, the home office isn't being used for work, the dining room isn't hosting anyone. When you add to that situation not being able to find what you are looking for and having to do multiple purchases, this puts a lot of stress on relationships between family members. The children feel they can't have friends over and the adults don't entertain. This creates a feeling of being trapped.

Organizing takes time. Busy people usually just start putting everything in the attic or basement. After that they hide everything in bins and drawers, but eventually those areas fill up, too. This isn't organization. **Being organized is different from being neat or tidy.**

Mollie: What circumstances led to your passion for simple living?

Ben: Growing up as a child of a difficult divorce, having control became pretty important to me. People have anxiety when they are not in control and in life there is a lot we cannot control; however, we can control our physical space. My belief is that **nothing good comes out of chaos** and being a minimalist and having organized systems allows me to be more productive. I see this with my own children: when their room is a mess they simply don't play in it, but **when the floor is clear they actually build things, use their toys and imagination.**

Also, as a child I always liked jigsaw puzzles. There's something about putting a giant mess together into something complete that calms the mind.

THE NAKED HOUSE

When I was young the desire for stuff seemed pretty cool but getting married and having children focuses you on experiences. A kid is excited by the new toy but she is also just as excited by the box it came in, and after a few hours it just goes on the pile with the other unused toys. The older you get you realize that happiness comes from within, that buying stuff doesn't solve your problems or actually make you happy. Having experiences with friends and family leads to great memories and at the end of the day, all we have are our memories.

Mollie: What are the common mistakes your clients make when it comes to managing their home environment?

Ben: For a lot of people, the act of shopping or the thrill of getting a bargain is the real juice and getting the thing is more important than the actual thing. Also, in our clients' homes we see items unused and crammed into closets and after reviewing we discover they are gifts the receiver didn't want, doesn't like and doesn't know what to do with.

Most people give gifts to make themselves, not the person getting it, feel better. If someone took the time to give something wanted it would be experiences or consumables; **a night of free babysitting is worth more than two hundred items from the Christmas Tree Shops or the Dollar Store**.

Mollie: Any additional tips for simplifying the home?

Ben: If you're a parent, you are the gatekeeper. When your kids are a certain age, they may get up to thirty or forty gifts for their birthdays and holidays. You know how your children play and what they like and steering people to give swimming lessons or tickets to the movies will save everyone in the end.

Another suggestions to cutting down on accumulating because of retail therapy is to pay cash for it. If you really want it, take the time to get cash out. You can also print the page out from Ebay or Amazon and wait a week. If you really still want it, then get it. My economics professor used to say, "More is preferred to less," but the stress of clutter hurts relationships and your free time and creates anxiety.

Mollie: One final thought?

Ben: Good things aren't cheap and cheap things aren't good. Well-made items that you can depend on are more important than quantity.

9

THE NAKED HOME CHECKLIST

AND NOW, as promised, the Naked Home checklist, including many of the action items mentioned in this book and some additional ones as well. A word of caution here first, though: don't let the process of cleaning and reorganizing feel tedious, and don't do something just because I recommend it. Have fun with this experience. Do what feels good to you. If possible, make reorganizing your home a hobby that you enjoy, and if that's not possible—well, do it less often but with a great deal more commitment.

You will not regret it.

First Things

- **Undertake a pre-purge evaluation.** First, picture your home completely clean and bare, with nothing inside it at all. Then, as you declutter, keep that image in mind.

- **Decide which room or space will accommodate your overflow.** This is the place your purge will start, in order to make room for more stuff.
- **Clearly identify your pantry and your office space, and which related item types will go in which.** This will save you tons of time from the start.
- **Purge, purge, and purge some more.** If you're really enthusiastic, you can first empty the room you're working in entirely, then bring back only the items that make the room better.
- **Start organizing.** This is something normally done in layers; no need to sort out each and every clothespin before you get your pantry drawer designations figured out.
- **Don't cram.** Keep all cabinets, particularly lower cabinets, under-full. Try not to store anything under the bed. Keep closet floors mostly bare.
- **Consider which furniture items can go.** When in doubt about a large item, haul it to the garage first—then see the difference not having it makes. Clearing out a few large things right off the bat is motivating. It also makes your workspace easier to access.
- **Choose your colors.** I recommend limiting yourself to three colors, plus black and white.
- **Choose your theme or era and your wood stain type.** No hurry here, but when you're purchasing new items, identifying your final look will be important.

THE NAKED HOUSE

- **Consider getting rid of the following items:** Lamps; lamp tables/end tables; fireplace pokers; knickknacks; dishes; books; toys; wall hangings; unmatching blankets, throws and sheets; coat racks; coffee tables; shelves, drawers and cabinets; heavy blinds and drapes; dressers; and bed frames. Also, make a good, honest assessment of each of your kitchen appliances.
- **Consider purchasing the following items:** A Rumba, matching storage baskets and boxes to use throughout the home, Pyrex and Correll dishes, bean bags and housekeeping services.
- When replacing the stuff you throw out, **choose plain, high-quality items that match the rest of the home.** When buying something in a set, buy a large amount.
- **When updating your home, keep simplicity and quality in mind.** Get thick, plush carpet. Buy better, not bigger or more. Don't buy cabinets with clear doors. Invest in quality lighting, flooring and paint.
- **Replace your hardware.** Get doorknobs, cabinet handles, sink fixtures, towel racks and vent covers that match.
- **Clear off your kitchen counters.** Entirely. All of your appliances should fit inside your cabinets.
- **Create a designated home for each of the following items:** The book or magazine you're currently reading; clothes you've worn once but want to wear again before washing; the outfit

you plan to wear tomorrow; remote controls; keys, wallets and purses; and letters waiting to be mailed. Some of these items are in my office and others are in a hanging shoe rack-turned-shelf in our hall closet.

- **When straightening up after a meal, leave the dishes for last.**
- **Move all of the bathroom and kitchen cleaners to a single, safe location.**
- **Clean out your bathroom cabinets,** and put everything not needed at least weekly in the garage.
- **Keep an in/out box near the garage door** (I call mine my "triage box") for items that you plan to return to the garage when time permits.
- **In the garage, create a "box wall,"** a single garage wall that is easily accessible and can accommodate small- to medium-sized everyday items. Label the boxes clearly and don't overfill them.
- **Scan and digitize all of your photos.**
- **Make the switch to ebooks.**
- If you have kids, **repurpose some of the stuff in garage into toys.**
- **Organize and purge some more.**

Naked Interview
Bernadette Joy Cruz: "My Husband and I Paid Off $300,000 of Debt in Three Years"

Bernadette Joy Cruz is a money media expert. She speaks and teaches about debt repayment and other financial issues and writes Crush Your Money Goals™.

Mollie: Tell me about your experience with minimalism.

Bernadette Joy: I've been in the process of decluttering and reorganizing my home as part of my journey to become debt-free. My husband and I paid off $300,000 of debt, including debt from student loans and two mortgages, in three years. Adopting a minimalist mindset was a big part of our change.

At first, I decided to declutter just to find things to sell in order to help pay off our debt. I sold a lot of unneeded housewares, clothing, furniture, etc. At the first garage sale we made over $400 in four hours and that encouraged me to want to get rid of more stuff because we weren't using any of it and it felt like free money!

Mollie: Tell me more about your debt repayment experience. How did you manage this feat? What did you give up?

Bernadette Joy: We started in January 2016 with about $70,000 in student loans and the rest in mortgages. It started because I felt overwhelmed with how much debt we accumulated in less than a two years because essentially, I cared more about what other people thought about us than about our own well-being. People will like me more if they think I'm smart and have a nice house, right? I started learning everything I could about money and debt through podcasts and YouTube. My husband and I started implementing everything I learned like budgeting and making extra money through side hustles. The biggest things we had to give up were time (we worked a lot during that time period), investing for the first 7 months (we stopped while we paid off the student loans and then resumed at 15% of our total income, more than what we were investing before) and large expenses like travel. All of this was temporary and since we've become debt free we've resumed all the conveniences and fun including going to see my favorite K-Pop band live in concert, buying a car in cash and going to Italy!

Mollie: What are your most prized beliefs regarding the minimalist lifestyle—the ideas you most want to spread?

Bernadette Joy: Minimalism is not just about stuff. It's about minimizing anything that causes you stress, including stress at work, stress in relationships and stress in your mind. I've worked on automating or outsourcing a lot of things that used to cause me stress (for example, I now have a regular cleaning service that helps me keep tidy instead of agonizing over not doing it myself). I also believe that you don't have to adopt a poor or no-fun lifestyle that I think people confuse with minimalism. I minimize material things like clothing and unnecessary house stuff to make room and finances available for things like going to concerts and on vacations.

Mollie: Can you share a few specific tips for organizing and simplifying?

Bernadette Joy: Find things you aren't using and sell them! Garage sales worked great for me in the area I'm in, but I also sold a lot of housewares on Facebook. It's a great way to encourage you if you're like me and feel guilty about what you spent; at least you make some money back and use the money towards something you really want.

Work on one room at a time only. Don't move onto the next room until you complete the previous. Start where you spend the most of your time because you will get the most benefit out of it. I started in my kitchen and in my bedroom. I immediately felt relief getting rid of so many kitchen items that were just cluttering up our space.

I'm a big fan of the minimalist challenge: get rid of one thing on the first day, two things on the second day, etc. for a month. I have committed to it at least once a year, sometimes multiple times a year. I like crossing things off my list and challenges in general and it really got me motivated to keep it up for a month!

Donate where you can instead of throwing stuff out. If I can't find local charities, I just post things for free on Facebook or Craigslist. Everything I've put out, someone has picked up, so at least I know (or hope) they are being reused!

Mollie: Any final thoughts on minimalism?

Bernadette Joy: For me, a minimalist mindset has not deprived me of anything I wanted. In fact, it's created more room for things I absolutely love in life and focused more on experiences than accumulating stuff. It's also always a work-in-progress. One might come to my house and not think it's minimalist because we own more than a few dishes or towels. But I can confidently say everything I own right now is on purpose and has a purpose, and that is peace of mind that I'm so grateful for.

APPENDIX ONE
MORE EXPERT ADVICE

From Adam Nathaniel Waitt of OneWipeWonders, a nutritional supplement company that helps people reduce toilet paper waste through healthy bowel movements (really!):

- "If you haven't used the thing in the past six months but think you'll miss it, you probably won't, so just get rid of it. If you end up missing it you can always get another. If you do later reacquire that item you will probably have deeper, healthier relationship with it."
- **"Get rid of flat surfaces where items can accumulate.** I used to have a bunch of shelves and tables which ended up getting cluttered. Now my living space only has surfaces that are needed and I am forced to put things back where they belong. Also, downsize your workshop/garage and **join a maker space.** It's like a gym for tools. You will probably have access to way more tools than you own now, you'll be

more intentional with your projects (and might actually get them done), and you'll become part of an awesome sharing community."

- "When struggling with getting rid of a certain item, try to be honest with yourself on why you value that thing. I often found that I was holding on to a thing for superficial reasons. For example, I once had a large collection of books that I displayed proudly for anyone who visited to see. I came to realize that I kept this collection more for the image they projected than for the information they contained. It was just displaying an insecurity. I have since recorded all of the books I was actually interested in reading using the Goodreads app. I kept a small selection of favorites but purged the rest. Now the library is my book collection."

From Brittany Ferri, an occupational therapist and a health writer at simplicityofhealth.com:

- "Some people prefer to delete social media from their phone so it isn't always with them. I wanted to go a step further and completely delete some apps like Snapchat while deactivating my Facebook. For Facebook, I thought perhaps one day I'd feel okay enough in my decluttering efforts all around to go back to it. However, I ended up loving how it felt to be disconnected from such a big platform as Facebook, so about a year ago (three years after my original declutter), I logged back in to delete it permanently. I found that replacing this social media wasn't entirely necessary, but I wanted to add something more productive to my life. So when I get the urge to mindlessly scroll through something on my phone, I pull up an ebook or get out a paperback to read."

- "My favorite tip on minimizing clutter is to **think about how the items in your life impact your life.** If you constantly find yourself stressed and drained in your home or work environments, this may be the change that improves your situation. If you still find yourself attached to many things and overwhelmed or upset at the prospect of decluttering, **you may have some soul searching or planning to do** before getting started."

- "I love minimizing clutter in areas where a lot of activity is needed. For example, living rooms are often meant to be cozy and have people around, so that may be a central area where most of your belongings are kept. Areas like a home office or kitchen are frequently used for work or cooking, and should be kept cleaner to allow for more efficiency."

From Amy Bloomer, founder of Let Your Space BLOOM:

- "My previous career was on Wall Street, so I love the idea of looking at the economics of becoming more of a minimalist. Let's face it, life is a numbers game. Investing in home organization does come at an initial cost. The good news is that it's a short-term investment that yields long-term dividends. I spent almost ten years postgraduate school living and working in Manhattan. Needless to say, space is at a very high premium in New York City. I had to learn to effectively and efficiently use every square inch of my apartment."

- "My favorite tip for simplifying a home is the following: **do not make decisions about individual things, until you've discovered and distributed each and every object into piles of similar categories.** If you try to make decisions each time you discover an object, you'll be forced to make the same decision, over and over again. Here's an example: let's say you are cleaning out a closet and discover 50 belts (trust me, I work with clients that have accumulated many more than that). Rather than make a decision about each belt you find when you find it, it's most efficient to wait until all of the belts have been discovered and distributed into a pile. This strategy has saved a lot of time and decision making brain power for my clients."

From Lisa Street Rogers, Co-Founder of Fast Lane Digital:

- "Three tips: First, **start with the paper.** Go through your paper stashes and throw out notes, old receipts, brochures you picked up but never looked at again, etc. Second, get rid of what's broken. Old electronics can be restored or traded in. Jewelry can be sold to crafters to make something new. Finally, pretend you're packing for a trip. Pack everything you think you'll need,

then take half of it out. Donate or sell what you take out. Rinse and repeat."
- "It's the experiences we have which help us live our lives to the fullest. Rather than spending money on the latest shining object, use it to experience the world. This doesn't just mean traveling. Take a class and learn something new. **Seek adventure.**"

From Sherri Monte of Elegant Simplicity (elegantsi.com):

- "As Nelson Mandela said, **"It always seems impossible until it is done."** If you're not 100 percent on board with or don't wholeheartedly believe that having a clutter-free home is possible then your actions will follow suit (as will the clutter!)."
- **"Break it down.** Do I use it and how often? When's the last time? Does it bring me joy? Do I love it? And, my personal favorite, do I need it? Seriously, think about what would happen if you got rid of it."
- **"Schedule maintenance.** Even the best of us who are living clutter-free and minimalist lifestyles accumulate possessions. Like anything in life, in order to maintain it, you have to take time to focus on it. Identify where things feel out of sync and schedule time to get clear on whatever is not working."

From Simon Hansen, founder and blogger at Family Travel Planet (familytravelplanet.com):

APPENDIX ONE

- "Don't get me wrong, I love Marie Kondō but if there's one thing I could disagree with, it's the belief that we have to get rid of things that no longer give us joy. I believe (and I know other people share this sentiment as well) that there are just some things in life that we need to keep no matter what it makes us feel. For example, the bills and the tons of reports on my desk give me little to no joy at all but it doesn't mean that I should throw it away. Being critical of the value of the things around us can make it easier for us to decide whether to keep it or not."

From David Nguy, a dentist living in Toronto, Canada (see atlas.dental):

- "The best thing about selling your things online is that it does not have to be a difficult or time-consuming process. I found that Kijiji makes an app that makes the experience easy and even fun. Taking Instagrammable, artsy photos of your things for sale, creating attractive and descriptive titles and descriptions can be fun. Making the sale can be very addictive, too, and is much preferable than throwing out in the trash and creating more landfill waste."
- "It is very easy to put things away in boxes, but if the boxes aren't properly labeled to identify what went into them, the objects inside can be easily forgotten. This creates more clutter, excess and waste. A general rule of thumb is that if the object cannot be easily seen, it doesn't exist. Avoid miscellaneous collection of things. They might as

well be thrown into the garbage. When organizing, use clear, see-through containers rather than opaque boxes. And make good use of masking tape and a sharpie marker."

Appendix Two: Recommended Reading

Action inspires more action, but books inspire action, too. Especially high-quality, practical books like these. My favorite tip comes from the great Marie Kondō: Throw out everything that doesn't give you a noticeable "spark of joy." Beautiful, and especially applicable to your clothes closet. If it doesn't make you feel good when you wear it and you can afford a few new clothes, no more guilt—just let it go.

Books on Reducing Home Clutter

The Life-Changing Magic of Tidying Up: The Japanese Art of Decluttering and Organizing, Marie Kondō

Goodbye, Things: The New Japanese Minimalism, Fumio Sasaki

Spark Joy: An Illustrated Master Class on the Art of Organizing and Tidying Up, Marie Kondō

A Life Less Throwaway: The Lost Art of Buying for Life, Tara Button

Essentialism: The Disciplined Pursuit of Less, Greg McKeown

The Joy of Less, A Minimalist Living Guide: How to Declutter, Organize, and Simplify Your Life, Francine Jay

Minimalism Memoirs

APPENDIX ONE

The Year of Less: How I Stopped Shopping, Gave Away My Belongings, and Discovered Life Is Worth More Than Anything You Can Buy in a Store, Cait Flanders

The 100 Thing Challenge: How I Got Rid of Almost Everything, Remade My Life, and Regained My Soul, Dave Bruno

Coming Clean: A Memoir, Kimberly Raw Miller

They Left Us Everything: A Memoir, Plum Johnson

A Field Guide to Happiness: What I Learned in Bhutan About Living, Loving, and Waking Up, Linda Leaming

You Can Buy Happiness (and It's Cheap): How One Woman Radically Simplified Her Life and How You Can Too, Tammy Strobel

What I Talk About When I Talk About Running, Haruki Murakami

Books on Reducing Life Clutter and Mind Clutter

The 30-Day Creative Morning Challenge, Evan Griffith

How to Relax, Thich Nhat Hanh

Whatever Arises, Love That: A Love Revolution That Begins with You, Matt Kahn

Dear reader,

We hope you enjoyed reading *The Naked House*. Please take a moment to leave a review, even if it's a short one. Your opinion is important to us.

Discover more books by Mollie Player at https://www.nextchapter.pub/authors/mollie-player

Want to know when one of our books is free or discounted? Join the newsletter at http://eepurl.com/bqqB3H

Best regards,

Mollie Player and the Next Chapter Team

You might also like:
Fights You'll Have After Having A Baby by Mollie Player

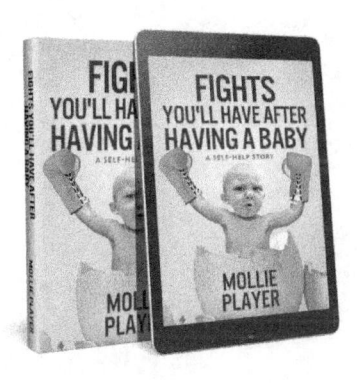

To read the first chapter for free, please head to:
https://www.nextchapter.pub/books/fights-youll-have-after-having-a-baby

ABOUT THE AUTHOR

Author and mental health counselor in training Mollie Player attempts feats of great strength, then writes about what happens. Her goals include: daily meditation, homeschooling her kids, not arguing with her spouse and, of course, finding inner peace. Her plans don't always work out, but when they do, the results are awesome. And when they don't, well, it keeps things interesting.

For more by Mollie Player, see her Amazon book page and mollieplayer.com.

CPSIA information can be obtained
at www.ICGtesting.com
Printed in the USA
LVHW082329131120
671658LV00020B/742

9 781715 757472